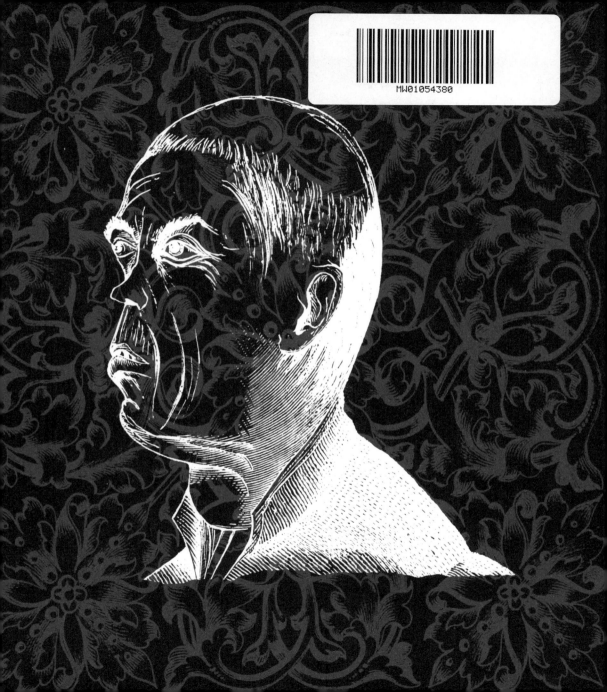

THE TUTU

Atlas Anti-Classics 19

First English edition of 2000 copies.

 LÉON GENONCEAUX
as Princess Sappho

THE TUTU

MORALS OF THE FIN DE SIÈCLE

Translated, introduced and with notes by Iain White

ATLAS PRESS LONDON 2013

Published by Atlas Press
BCM ATLAS PRESS, LONDON WC1N 3XX
Translation ©2013 Iain White
©2013 Atlas Press
A CIP catalogue for this book is available from
The British Library
ISBN: 1-900565-63-3
ISBN-13: 978-1-900565-63-9
Printed and bound by CPI, Chippenham.
USA distribution: Artbook/DAP
www.artbook.com
UK distribution: Turnaround
www.turnaround-uk.com

CONTENTS

There are things it would be pleasant to believe... though there are limits to credibility. All the same, the wish — or perhaps the possibility — persists...

In *Ulysses*[1] we read of how Stephen Dedalus, summoned from Paris for his mother's funeral, brought back with him "Rich booty [...] *Le Tutu*, five tattered numbers of *Pantalon Blanc et Culotte Rouge*". Whether or not Joyce might have known, seen or heard of the book *Le Tutu* is still — just about — an open question. It seems probable that the *Le Tutu* mentioned here was only a short-lived cheap-and-cheerful and faintly "racy" magazine. Joyce's biographer Frank Budgen in *The Making of Ulysses* mentions the writer's affectionate knowledge of an analogous publication, *Photo Bits*; and then there was Poldy and Molly Bloom's predilection for *Sweets of Sin*... But then again, Joyce was a voracious and omnivorous reader, and well acquainted with French *fin-de-siècle* writing... There are things it would be pleasant to believe...

However, Joyce's knowing of this book would have made him quite unique. For a long time, indeed until its centennial republication in 1991, *Le Tutu* could have been described as the book that almost never was. It simply vanished. It was published in the autumn of 1891, but somehow or other, nobody knows how,

1. On p.42 of the Oxford World's Classics edition.

when, or why, save for a few copies, nearly the whole of the print-run seems to have just disappeared. If we are to believe an announcement in the eminently respectable *Bibliographie de la France* for 6 June 1891, the author of this forthcoming work was a certain "Sapho" (in its French spelling), and its publisher was Léon Genonceaux. The two would appear to be identical: Sapho was almost certainly Genonceaux, and Genonceaux was almost certainly Sapho.

It was in April 1966 that *Le Tutu* briefly resurfaced in an article by Pascal Pia[2] in *Le Quinzaine littéraire*. In this article Pia's initial aim was to praise Genonceaux as one of those he called the "inventors" of Lautréamont and Rimbaud, drawing attention to the "two master-strokes Genonceaux accomplished in less than a year: first, in December 1890, by republishing *Les Chants de Maldoror*,[3] then, in November 1891, assembling under the title *Reliquaire*, the poetry of Rimbaud". Pia goes on to quote the critic Maurice Saillet who described Genonceaux as "a hero of publishing", as "a rather picaresque individual", and as "one of those adventurers of the book, hounded by the police and by creditors". The same article mentions the possible existence of a manuscript of memoirs by Genonceaux sold at auction in Brussels in 1948. The purchaser has never been identified; but if the manuscript — still? — exists it might well throw some light on the genesis of *Le Tutu*.

Pia goes on to reveal that it was "only by pure chance" that he came upon a copy

2. Pascal Pia (1903-79) *né* Pierre Durand: a Great War orphan; autodidact, poet and literary scholar; journalist; active fighter in the Resistance; editor of Apollinaire, Baudelaire, Cros and Lautréamont; specialist in *livres interdits* and in literary hoaxes; pataphysician.
3. Pia rather underplays Genonceaux's contribution here. He published *Maldoror* in France for the first time. The previous edition had appeared in Belgium to evade censorship, and as a consequence went unnoticed; it was only with the French publication that the work began to acquire its reputation.

of *Le Tutu*. This is unsurprising, since even now there are only five known copies of the first edition, none of them in libraries.[4] Having meticulously retyped the entire text, he tried time and again to interest potential publishers. To no avail... It was only twelve years after Pia's death that, in 1991, a small provincial publishing house took the risk of presenting this oddity to readers.

Pia's summary of what he called "this gallery of eccentrics, of extravagants, indeed monsters, in the literal sense of the term" was brief and exact, and surely tempting enough to appeal to potential readers. The characters are grotesque for good reasons: *Le Tutu* is both a *roman à clef* (a "you-know-whom" novel) as well as a *roman à deux sous* (a "penny dreadful"), and, as Pia points out, "it is a novel which is not devoid of malice". Genonceaux had motives enough for malice it seems for he was dealt a pretty unlucky hand with regards to his career in publishing. Not all the victims of his barbed wit are now identifiable (and luckily the novel's power does not depend on these long-past disputes). The hero, however, certainly is: in real life Mauri de Noirof was Maurice de Brunhoff or Brunof.[5] This individual, born in 1861 in Wiesbaden, was the son of a Swedish industrialist who — like Mauri de Noirof's father — died in a railway accident. Having acquired a diploma in engineering he soon moved over into publishing, first in association with the respectable Édouard Monnier, then with the Librairie Piaget. The policy adopted by these publishers was to bring out "proper" literature

4. One of these copies lacks a cover, and another has scrawled on its title-page the inscription: "*Dégoutant, à brûler*" — "Disgusting, to be burnt".

5. Other characters may also be identified. Jardisse, the camel-hump-nosed swindler, is fairly clearly one of Genonceaux's authors, Henri d'Argis, author of *Sodome*, dedicated to and prefaced by Verlaine. Madame Perle may well, in real life, have been a then well-known hostess reputed to dispense political and other favours from her boudoir — and whose actual preferences, however, tended towards the sapphic.

subsidised by more libidinous works — just as Genonceaux was later to do. A contemporary photograph shows Brunhoff to have been the spitting image of Mauri de Noirof: "tall, thin, beard trimmed to a point, eyes black…".

Belgian by origin, and born in 1856, Genonceaux began his own publishing career working for Brunhoff and his associates or successors before founding his own business on the Rue Saint-Benoit in 1890. As noted above, his publishing programme resembled that of his past employers, racy novels interspersed with more literary offerings: Huysmans, Lautréamont, Rimbaud, Michelet — and Rachilde, who rather straddled the two categories.

The manuscript of *Le Tutu* is dated 26 September 1891, but Genonceaux had announced the book in June, so the date in September probably indicated when it was about to go to print (as its publisher he would have been able to make changes up to then). Unfortunately it was exactly at this moment that his problems with the authorities came to a head.

His rather impulsive publication of Rimbaud's poems had aroused the anger of the book's editor, Roland Darzens, who claimed that his preface had been printed without permission. Darzens began legal action, and soon after the book's appearance at the beginning of November the police seized all the undistributed copies they could lay hands upon. When Genonceaux produced a second edition only a week later, without the preface, this too was confiscated, this time because the corrected preface had been omitted. The authorities struck again soon afterwards, seizing in Cherbourg copies of a third-rate piece of would-be erotica called *Hémine* by one Jean Larocque. The book was quickly traced to Genonceaux and most of the print-run was discovered at his binders in Paris and confiscated.

 Genonceaux was taken into custody, briefly, in all likelihood, and charged with publishing an immoral work. The authorities appeared to be serious

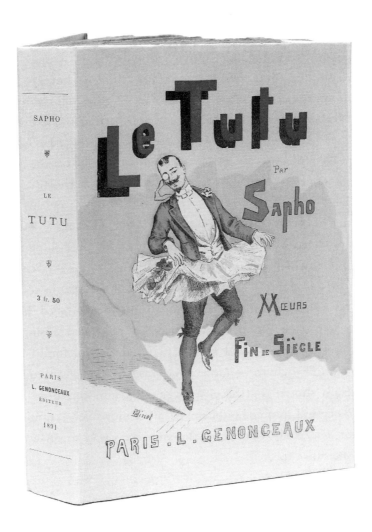

Our thanks to Pierre Saunier for this photograph of the finest known copy of the first edition.

and Genonceaux went on the run (according to a letter from Verlaine to his publisher dated 19 November).

Le Tutu was printed immediately after *Reliquaire*, and it would certainly have been unwise to put out a book which was not only obscene, but also blasphemous, under these circumstances. It is perhaps this fact — above all the others listed in the sources given at the end of this Introduction — that is the most persuasive piece of evidence that Genonceaux was indeed the author of *Le Tutu*: he had to abandon his publishing business just at the moment it came off the press. Had the author been someone else, who did not have to flee the authorities at such short notice, then there would surely be more trace of the book from this time.

The sequence of events then becomes a little vague. Genonceaux was eventually charged and convicted *in absentia* in January 1892 for publishing another book altogether, *Zé Boïm*, which was judged to have an obscene cover. The sentence was 13 months in prison and a 3,000-franc fine (around £10,000 in today's money). Genonceaux, however, had escaped the country and he resurfaced the same year at an address in London's Bloomsbury, where he produced a single issue of a magazine devoted to unpublished French material he had found in the British Museum Library. (The trip to London cannot have been his first, judging from the extreme revulsion shown for the city in chapter 8 of this novel.) In 1903 he returned to France and resumed publishing, rather more discreet publications than previously, but after only two years this venture came to an end. Thereafter nothing. Genonceaux vanished.

---

6. A need that in part explains the book's cover, with its inappropriate gaiety. It is, in fact, a pastiche of the cover of a pseudonymous work by Brunhoff, *Paris sur scène* by Guy de Saint-Môr, published by Piaget when Genonceaux worked for him. The cover features a ballerina in a tutu with a red chemise, just as the cover of *Le Tutu* depicts a recognisable Brunhoff

The circumstances of the composition of *Le Tutu*, so partially known (why such a pressing need to get a rise out of Brunhoff, for instance?),[6] do not really explain much about it, except circumstantially. Genonceaux appears to have attempted to write the "decadent novel" to end all decadent novels. With this aim in mind, and that of appalling his readers *à la Lautréamont*, he employed a combination of French literary genres — popular fiction, science fiction (or "anticipatory fiction" as it was known then), Romantic horror ("frenetics" in France, a sort of equivalent to the Grand Guignol theatre of the time), "one-handed" literature (such as he had published, but given extra refinements here, to say the least), all embraced within a distinctly Symbolist aesthetic. Genonceaux's hero appears, at first anyway, rather similar to those of Huysmans, Bloy or Lorrain — Mauri is a youthful aesthete, something of a dandy, a disillusioned narcissist unable to reconcile himself with his times. He differs by the fact that, whereas these earlier writers made of such a character a morbid neurasthenic, Genonceaux instead indulges his hero with a cheerful relishing of every imaginable perversity. Perhaps we can see here the influence of Rimbaud's call from the end of *A Season in Hell*: "We must be absolutely modern." Genonceaux's book is above all forward-looking; its hero invents fantastic machines and gleefully casts aside an old morality, but its modernity is embedded deeper than such surface elements. When one compares this work to its nearest English equivalent, Wilde's *The Picture of Dorian Gray*, the contrast could not be more striking. These books were written within a year of one another, but Wilde's conventionally plotted entertainment could not be more different from the furiously reckless invention of Genonceaux's half-crazy book in

in a tutu and wearing a red jacket. The episode involving the tutu in the book evidently had a hidden meaning that Brunhoff would (probably not) have appreciated. The pseudonym of Sapho (or Sappho in its English spelling), remains a mystery, however, in a book singularly devoid of lesbianism!

which he crashed together almost every known literary genre.

Borges famously proposed that literary works create their own precursors by showing connections between earlier writers that were previously unrecognised. Genonceaux's book presents a more extreme paradox, in that it seems more to resemble works that came *after* it. As Goytisolo noted: "We find in it a clear presentiment (one cannot say influence, since no one read this book) of the audacities of Jarry, Roussel, Breton, Ionesco, Queneau". This list of names could be easily extended, and yet it is true that Genonceaux's book had no influence whatsoever. Which leaves us with an unanswerable question: what effect would it have had if it had indeed appeared in 1891, when it was written?

Sources:

"Princesse Sapho", *Le Tutu*, Léon Genonceaux, Paris, 1891; reprinted by Tristram, Mayenne, 1991 and 2008 (with an afterword, "Quel livre étrange…" by Jean-Jacques Lefrère).

Pascal Pia, "Un des inventeurs Maldoror", *La Quinzaine littéraire*, 15 April 1966 available at http://laquinzaine.wordpress.com/2011/04/18/un-de-des-inventeurs-maldoror/

Jean-Jacques Lefrère & Jean-Paul Goujon, *Deux malchanceux de la littérature fin de siècle: Jean Larocque et Léon Genonceaux*, Du Lérot, Tusson, 1994 (the best source on Genonceaux).

"Princesa Safo", *El Tutú*, preface by Juan Goytisolo, Blackie Books, Barcelona, 2009.

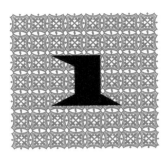

When he found himself in the street a fine, persistent rain, comparable to powdered water and so fine, so fine that it scarcely fell, so that it was difficult to determine whether it was coming from on high or rising up from the ground, an impalpable rain, like liquefied air-molecules, was cloaking the boulevard in a mist the gas lamps had trouble in penetrating. In something of a daze, Mauri de Noirof set off at random, halted, turned on his heels, and resumed his irregular progress, in his mind a vague recollection of *the thing* he had just for the first time done. He caught sight of a fragment of brick on the asphalt and it amused him to propel it in front of him with little kicks; the stone rolled leftwards or to the right according to its humour. This bit of brick came to interest him; he picked it up, and immediately gave a start: a strident sound blazed out above his head. It was a train leaving for Brittany. The steam from the engine, denser than the atmosphere, masked the string of carriages and slowly descended to be engulfed under the arches of the railway-bridge. Mauri got his bearings. He could not be far from the Gare Montparnasse. Stories of ruffians then flooded back into his memory and, for fear of being murdered, he retraced his steps, regained the left-hand pavement of the Boulevard de Montrouge, his piece of brick still in his hand. Where did it come from, this fragment of baked earth? What had become of the great-grandfather of the worker who had wielded the first, the very first pickaxe to penetrate the clay from which it was to be moulded? Who had left it there, on the pavement? Had it a soul, this morsel of brick? Was it troubled by the rain, or the heat? Mauri was wrenched from these reflections by the passage of a lamplighter extinguishing the street-lamps with two or three drawn-out *pssts* at his back. At that very moment he remembered an evening he had spent, five years previously, in the house of a friend of his mother's, in the Doubs. Next the idea of eating snails without garlic, on a headless horse that would take the bit between its teeth backwards, obsessed him. Then he stumbled against another bit of brick, which he set rolling in front of him, again with little kicks. He walked slowly, carefully avoiding the lines between the flagstones; this amused him. At one point he trod on one of the lines, and was vexed at his clumsiness. A workman overtook him; Mauri noticed that the seat of his trousers was wrinkling into a grimace. After that he did not think of anything. His head emptied under that May rain which was slowly freezing him, seeping through the new clothes which he had put on freshly, for the third time that day.

Before going down the Rue d'Odessa he turned around; the house had an imposing air, its shutters closed as religiously as a virgin's eyes. Although there was nothing particularly remarkable about its architecture, it was *the most beautiful* house on the boulevard. For all that, the building resembled all the other buildings: no matter, it was the most beautiful. Further *pssts* made themselves heard.

"Monsieur Mauri, you're letting me go, then?"

"Ah! So it's you? What are you doing there?"

"But I'm waiting for you of course! You said you'd only be a minute."

Mauri stared at him.

"You're drenched, Pancrace; yes, God bless us, drenched. Me too, what's more. What vile weather! Ah, so you've waited for me all night... But that's stupid, you only had to go in and ask for me."

"I was afraid I'd disturb you. Anyhow, it would have cost me nineteen francs..."

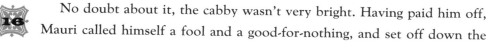 No doubt about it, the cabby wasn't very bright. Having paid him off, Mauri called himself a fool and a good-for-nothing, and set off down the

Rue d'Odessa, looking for a café where he could flop, for he was experiencing a strange weariness in his legs. This weariness in his legs astonished even him; and, quite deliberately, he resolved not to consider its causes.

"Monsieur Mauri, my cab, eh?"

These words emerged from the windpipe of a second cabby, this time from the Urbaine — the first was from the Coopérative, or rather the Métropolitaines. He was demanding fifteen francs for having waited since midnight.

"That's right, Monsieur Mauri, since midnight. You told me yesterday to come and wait for you at midnight. I've been waiting for you since midnight. It's five o'clock. Work it out for yourself!"

"…ugger off, will you! That's the last time I'll be taking any cabs. When I book them, I don't use them. I'll do like everybody else, and make do with buses."

"But at night, Monsieur Mauri…"

The cabby was right, there were no buses at night-time. He offered the man a drink, which the man refused with dignity. On top of that there was no café on the Rue d'Odessa, and no establishment on the Place de Rennes was open. Noirof strolled off, splashing through yellow puddles, wet as a duck, still intrigued by the piece of brick, which he had not discarded. A few rare passers-by cast him curious glances, and a policeman eyed him contemptuously. Where to go? The half-hour chimed on the station clock. Five-thirty! He, Mauri de Noirof, out on the street at that hour! He turned back, but since he had a horror of passing by the same place twice in succession — he considered this a locomotionary pleonasm — he turned down the Rue du Départ, feeling troubled by the memory of a cigar that had made him unwell, six months ago, at Madame Perle's, the *grande cocotte* of the Champs Élysées, where the games were played for high stakes. Yes, that cigar had made him unwell. All at once he was back on the Boulevard de Montrouge and, by a curious chance, all the morning's events became involved in a disorderly round-dance in his brain: setting out, the piece of brick, the train-whistle, the railway-bridge, the foot that trod on a line between the flagstones, the other piece of brick, the two cabbies, the tiredness in his legs. The day was having trouble dawning, the too-heavy mist remained birdlimed to the ground; the air stank of water; workmen were emerging from the Rue de la Gaîté and costermongers were setting up their stalls on the boulevard. Everything was dreary. Noirof's eyes felt tired; every time he blinked he seemed to feel grains of sand rolling under his eyelids. A funny business, this life! Last night he had known the ultimate delight, there in that big house that was still chastely asleep. It was there — the ideal of the flesh! He hesitated: should he go back home, at such an unaccustomed hour, or should he not? Where to take refuge? Soaked as he was, where to go and dry out? He was shivering. He passed an antique-dealer's shop window and looked at his reflection; this must have been the first time he'd caught sight of himself since he was genuinely astonished at what he saw. Was that him, that lanky and watery carcass with a face verging upon the green-drowned-man's-corpse-that's-spent-three-months-in-the-water, with that crookedly knotted necktie, the buttons of his overcoat through the buttonholes of his waistcoat, and streaks of rain down his cheek — and mucky all over? He said to himself:

"I look like a tramp; I shall give myself a couple of *sous*."

With his right hand he found a *sou* in his waistcoat pocket and generously presented it to himself.

"There you are, old fellow, it's the thought that counts."

This monologue raised a smile, and he smiled kindly upon himself, and he felt a contentment which he formulated thus, in an undertone, or rather in the voice of a prostrate man with his chest oppressed by a good few million kilogrammes:

"Jolly splendid, what!"

Then he made up his mind: he wouldn't be going back home this morning. At a cracking pace he crossed the boulevard and went back into the brothel.

2

Now that he had known *that*, an idea was tormenting him. Hitherto the chastity of his life had closed off mysteries to him. That night spent in the brothel was opening up new horizons. He told himself that with a name like his, and an engineer's diploma in his pocket, he could take a risk and find a wife. He suffered none the less from an indecisive character; he got headaches, and his memory was unfaithful to him. It was so unfaithful that he often spent hours on end in a state of profound stupefaction; he no longer remembered his own name. He inherited this from his father who, one day, forgot to live, as a result of a minor injury inflicted by a locomotive running over his body. This accident brought the widow three or four hundred thousand francs in damages, an unexpected fortune that enabled her to *send her son to a boarding-school* and give him *a good education*. Mauri — short for Maurice — took his classes at the State School of Civil Engineering, where he distinguished himself in nothing whatsoever. He learnt nothing, and qualified as an engineer. When he left the school, he entered the brothel. When he left the brothel, he wanted back in. No, that wasn't reasonable. Better to get married: he'd raise the matter that very day with his mother. The latter lived a stone's throw from the Arc de Triomphe in a little mezzanine flat, very homely, very comfortable. She was a tall woman, unlettered but distinguished, with a mania for old furniture and who managed her fortune very badly. In her ignorance she took an interest above all in those sciences concerned with the exploitation of mines. It was for that reason that her son Mauri had studied at the School of Civil Engineering. When he returned, worn out, from the Boulevard de Montrouge, she merely said: "You're a ruined man," and didn't weep at all. She in no way reproached him; everything was very dignified. For his part, he stretched out on a chaise-longue, stammered a bit and invented a story about spending the night with students in the cellars of Les Halles to celebrate the anniversary of the death of one of their fellows in the proper manner.

"We had a little fun, you know. There was no end of odd people there, tarts, hooligans, literary types. We kicked up a shindy. It's the first time something like that has happened to me; you have to start somewhere." Then he said:

"I have a feeling I had something to tell you."

And he searched about in his head, listening absent-mindedly to what his mother was telling him, making gestures of denial to the questions she put to him.

"So they don't teach you anything, then, at the Civil Engineers' School? Come now, you could at least give me an answer: that's only fair. At all events it's new. The Comte d'Esbignabrougne has put fifty thousand francs into it, Monsieur Possute as well. What do you think of it?"

At that moment a young man entered. His nose was the first thing one noticed, it was a nose the shape of a camel's hump, bulky, long, red and enormous, a nose capable of containing a tipcart-load of snotdrops. At equal distances from that nose there extended narrow ears which seemed to want to detach themselves from his head. Neither moustache nor beard. The absence of incisors gave his mouth the appearance of the muzzle of a toothless guinea-pig and, when he spoke, his nose crinkled up as if in a grimace. He gesticulated affectedly, his index finger always raised, and his get-up was very casual.

He explained his plan.

"I need a hundred and fifty thousand francs, not a centime less. The extraction of gold from the paving-stones of Paris* is one of the finest conceptions of the human spirit. But initially it may be necessary to lay out a hundred francs in labour costs to obtain a centime's worth of gold. Later the business will run itself. I can assure you that it will run itself. This certainty is based on Chemical analyses, which are indisputable. Here, in any case, is the report of the Academy of Sciences in Copenhagen, dated 17 March 1801. It is in Danish; would you like me to translate it for you?"

Mauri broke in here. He had got the point. In his capacity as an engineer he backed the claims of the camel-nosed man. There was undoubtedly gold in the paving-stones of Paris. Not much, perhaps, but certainly a little.

"You have a splendid idea there, Monsieur."

"Yes," the man replied, "truly splendid. For my part I have always tried to practise the following principle: to live and make money without taking any risks and working as little as possible. Be assured, I'm not forcing you to become a partner in my business; I have an idea, I pass it on to you; if it seems good, and if you put capital into it, we're making an exchange, and we're quits. You're taking a risk, it's a question of having a shot at it; tough luck if you lose… It's clear, isn't it, that you won't lose anything. The Comte d'Esbignabrougne, a shrewd individual, turned his thoughts round seven hundred and seventy-seven times in his head before making up his mind. Now see for yourself and judge. I'm here, Madame, because you were telling me about your son, whom you wanted to consult first. But, as it happens, this must be the gentleman, whom I knew at boarding-school with the Juilly brothers."

"Jardisse!"

"Noirof!"

In truth, the two were school-friends. Jardisse, a failure, having tried his hand at medicine then started up in the antiques trade, where he had managed to get through a hundred thousand francs in travel and dissipation. So he had to shut up shop, a dismal and damp little business in the Rue Jacob, and try something else. His family, whose outmoded cast-offs made up the whole of his wardrobe, stopped his allowance. Reading in the newspapers the marriage announcements and spiels of shady financiers, he dreamed of exploiting human stupidity. With Stupidity being eternal, there will always be a way to exploit it. The Creator, if there is one, made an error of omission when he drew out of nothingness the first man and the first woman: he forgot not to make them in his own image. He thereby condemned himself forever more to having before his eyes the photograph of his own image — stupid people. The Good Lord is too highly regarded to be taken for a ride; otherwise that would surely have come about. But, since he is unapproachable, one must fall back on his creatures. Thus reasoned Jardisse. The gold in the paving-stones of Paris offered a propitious terrain. And Madame de Noirof ploughed fifty thousand francs into it.

 ## THE HEARTACHE

ONE ACT, IN PROSE
Characters: Mme de Noirof; Mauri de Noirof, her son

The action takes place in the Rue de Presbourg, by the junction of the Arc de Triomphe. Comfortably-off interior. Splendid weather. The trees are in flower.

SHE: You're backing me up?

HE: I believe you. You're going to decuple your dosh.

SHE, *irritated*: Dosh?

HE: It's slang for money.

SHE: I was aware of that. So use other expressions. What's the matter with you, fidgeting about like that?

HE: It's just that I had something to tell you, but I can't remember what it was any more.

SHE: Even so, you agree with me, don't you, that Monsieur Jardisse's idea is splendid?

HE: Oh, yes indeed; but you've got to be on your guard: he's a rotter.

SHE: So much the better. And you, my dear, what have you decided on?

HE: Just look out there, at that magnificent chestnut tree!

SHE: Yes, it's a...

HE: Oh, it's lovely!

SHE, *nonplussed*: So then? (*She opens her eyes very wide, vacant as the vacant lot outside.*)

HE: I'm barmy, I'd like to be in love with matter. (*At this point he fidgets about, fumbles in a back pocket, pulls out the piece of brick.*) There, that's what was bothering me. Ah! Heavens above! I remember. You know what I'd really like?

SHE: What?

HE: To get married. I've been thinking about marriage since this morning. I should like to marry something that wasn't a human being.

SHE: A tipcart?

HE: No — people don't marry tipcarts. A tree, for example, like that chestnut tree. Oh, to bed a tree! Make it pregnant! Have children with it!

SHE, *placidly*: And go out with it to a nice quiet afternoon tea with the President of the Republic?

HE: Are you joking? Did I ask to live? Was I consulted before being brought into the world? I wasn't, was I? So, if I exist, it's none of my doing, and, if

I exist, am I obliged to submit to the laws the human herd has imposed upon itself, without asking my permission? Must I do what everybody else does? You go on about my marrying a tree! Yes, without any doubt, I'd certainly marry a tree.

SHE: The parents would have to agree.

HE: If need be I'd make the necessary formal request for permission. Come now, you want me to be frank with you, to lay my soul bare, open my heart to you, lay it bare to you? The world's in a stupor. It's only the two of us who really understand each other: shall we get married?

SHE: No, you're too stupid. If I agreed to legal cohabitation with your father, it was because I recognised in him certain qualities that you lack.

HE: I beg you, let's get married. Oh, to love one's saintly trollop of a mother! Bed her! Make her pregnant!

SHE: Be off with you, child!

HE: Why, though? All women disgust me, except you. Young ladies of fifteen to thirty disgust me too. Little girls of seven to fifteen are too artful. You want me to have a relationship with a kid of three or five?

SHE: Wouldn't a little boy of a couple of days be preferable?

HE: None of your profanity!

SHE: If anyone were to take down our conversation there'd be an outcry.

HE: You have such advanced ideas, it's a pleasure to talk to you. Out of a thousand women, there wouldn't be another like you. I've acknowledged your superiority; I shall put on unwhipped-cream gloves and ask for your hand in marriage.

SHE: But, you imbecile, you know full well the law doesn't allow of that.

HE: I expected as much, of course. Very well then, find me a wife.

SHE: Who? Do you suppose people get married like that, full speed ahead?

HE: Yes. I need a wife right away. You'll marry us *à la* Reclus.* After that we won't give it another thought.

(*She ponders briefly, a hand shading her eyes. He looks thoughtfully at his piece of brick.*)

SHE: Fanny Pompeux?*

HE: No. She's too thin. On top of that, she splutters when she speaks.

SHE: Sophie Puceau?*

HE: Not her either. She has bad breath.

SHE: Claire Noir?

HE: Too much of a podge!

SHE: Podge?

HE: Too fat, of course. I have a horror of fat women.

SHE: Why?

HE: And thin ones too.

SHE: But why?

HE: The fat ones go you-know-where too often, and the thin ones not enough.

SHE: Too often where?

HE: You want me to spell it out for you?

SHE: I don't understand.

HE: You've seen fat women before, very fat ones. You've seen them when they walk. Their backsides wobble like bags of gelatine. Why's that?

SHE: How should I know?

HE: Because such women are stuffed full of faeces…

SHE: Oh!

HE: … and gut-rumbling. They're bloated with gut-rumbling. And they let out silent farts at the drop of a hat.

SHE: What do you know about it?

HE: I'm quite convinced of it. So now, that's distinctly disagreeable. As for the thin ones, it's the other way round: they have nothing in their bellies.

When they go to the privy — and they only go every four or five or six or seven or eight days — they have trouble depositing even a few little black, dry and hard goat-turds that drop silently, one at a time, like bullets. And, if you were a man, would you spend your life with a woman like that! Never in a lifetime. I must have a happy medium.

SHE, *entranced*: What a man! We'll find you one though, you rascal. For all that you're a badly brought-up sort of a fellow.

HE: You're right there, but whose fault is that?

SHE: Ours, evidently. Children today are educated in a ridiculous fashion; we hide life from them and, when they begin to get a glimpse of it, they are prim and proper and know nothing about it. Prejudices must be abolished; we all suffer from them. Take me, when I got married, I knew nothing of men. Well now, that's stupid. Once past the age of twelve, little boys and girls ought to have intimate relations, but all that, naturally enough, is subordinate to climate. Children born under a southern sky, for example in Spain, ought to be familiar with each other at seven or eight. Those hatched at the equator ought to get to know each other in their mothers' wombs.

HE: God almighty, mother, you really are a caution!

SHE, *ingenuously*: Don't take the piss, Mauri. You were talking just now about the trouble with women going to the privy; that's not nice, you shouldn't stir such things up. (*A pause of fifteen to seventeen seconds.*) You're right, all the same — the best things return to matter. The most beautiful of women are only composed, chemically speaking, of the quintessence of faecal matter.

HE: Exactly. And this has even been the subject of a truly remarkable correspondence between the Duchesse d'Orléans and the Electrice of Saxony.* I shall read it to you. (*He goes to his room and returns with a book. He reads.*)

The Duchesse d'Orléans to the Electrice of Saxony

Fontainebleau, 9 October 1694

You are very fortunate to be able to go and shit when you want to; so carry on shitting to your heart's content. Things are not the same for us here, where I am obliged to bake my turd until the evening; there are no frottoirs* in the houses here in the forest. I have the misfortune to live in such a house, and, as a consequence, have the annoyance of having to go and shit out of doors, which grieves me because I like to shit at my ease, and I do not shit at my ease when my arse is not supported. Item, everybody can see us shitting; men, women, girls, boys go by, abbés and Switzers;* from this one must conclude that there is no pleasure without pain, and that if one did not shit I would be in my element in Fontainebleau. It is most vexing that my pleasures should be thwarted by turds; I wish that whoever it was who first invented shitting, that he and all his breed could only shit when beaten with cudgels. How, damn it! would it be possible to live without shitting? Be you at table with the best of company that might be, let the need to shit come upon you, then shit you must. Be you with a pretty girl, with a woman that pleases you, let the need to shit come upon you, shit you must or die. Ah, damnèd shitting! I know of no more scurvy a thing than shitting. You see a pretty young thing go by, very dainty, very clean, and you cry out within yourself: Ah! how comely she would be if she did not shit! I pardon it in porters, in soldiers, in watchmen, in chairmen and in people of that order. But emperors shit, empresses shit, the pope shits, cardinals shit,

27

princes shit, archbishops and bishops shit, the generals of religious orders shit, curés and parish priests shit. Admit, then, that the world is filled with scurvy creatures for, in the end, they shit in the air, they shit on the land, they shit in the sea, the entire universe is filled with shitters and the streets of Fontainebleau are filled with shit, for here they shit turds as big as yourself, Madame. You may think you are kissing a pretty little mouth with teeth so very white, but you are kissing a shit-mill; and the most delicate of dishes, biscuits, patés, tarts, partridges, hams, pheasants, all of them serve only to make softened shit, &c.

The Electrice's reply

Hanover, 31 October 1694

This is an agreeable argument you have constructed on the subject of shitting, though it seems that you know scarcely any of its pleasures, since you make no mention of what shitting has to offer in this regard; such is the worst of your misfortunes. One must have never shat in one's lifetime for the pleasure of shitting not to be known; for one might argue that, of all the necessities to which nature has subjected us, that of shitting is the most pleasant. One encounters few shitters who do not find that their turd smells sweet; the greater proportion of maladies come to us only through lack of shitting, and physicians cure us primarily by aiding us to shit: he who shits best, heals soonest. It might indeed be said that we eat only to shit, and similarly that we shit only to eat, and, if meat makes us shit, it is also true that the shit makes the meat, since the most delicious pork is from pigs that eat the most shit. At the most refined of tables, is not shit served in stews? Is there not shit in their roasts of woodcock, snipe, larks and other birds, whose shit serves as a side-dish to revive the appetite? Are not boudins, andouilles *and other sausage nothing but stews* stuffed into sacs à merde? Would not the soil become sterile if we did not shit, since it produces the finest and most delicate and necessary of dishes only by dint of turds and shit? It being still an acknowledged truth that whoever is able to shit on his own field will not go and shit on another's. The most beautiful women are those who shit the best; those who do not shit become dried-up and skinny, and as a result ugly. The most beautiful complexions are maintained only by frequent clysters which promote shitting; it is therefore to shit that we are obliged for our beauty. Physicians write the most learned of dissertations only with the aid of the shit of the sick; have they not transported from India an infinity of drugs which serve only to make us shit? Shit enters into the most exquisite of pomades and rouges. Without the shit of martens, civets and other animals, would we not be deprived of the most savoury and potent scents? The babies that shit the most in their swaddling-clothes are the whitest and the plumpest. Shit is an ingredient in many remedies, in particular those for burns and scalds. Agree, then, that shitting is the most handsome, the most useful, and the most pleasant thing in the world. When one does not shit, one feels heavy, out of sorts and ill-humoured. After shitting, one becomes lively, cheerful, and can eat with zest. Eating and shitting, shitting and eating, these acts follow and succeed one another, and it might easily be concluded that one eats only to shit just as one shits only to eat. You must have been in a *thoroughly bad humour when you inveighed so against shitting; I would not venture to hazard the reason unless it were assuredly that your waistband, being double-knotted, had caused you to shit in your hose. In short you are at liberty to shit when and wherever the spirit moves you, you should have no concern for anybody; the pleasure you procure for yourself in shitting shall so titillate you that, without regard for the place in which you find yourself, you shit in public, you shit on another's doorstep without being troubled whether or not he finds it proper and, mark that this pleasure, being for the shitter less shameful than for those who see him shit, that the convenience and the pleasure are the shitter's alone. I hope that now you will think better of considering shitting in so bad an odour, and that you will henceforth be of the opinion that one would as well not live at all, as not shit at all.*

HE: That's jolly nicely put, or I'm no judge of the matter.

SHE: Let's get back to the point. You want to get married. And your position?

HE: Well now, I'll form a partnership with the director of the Librairie du Marais, a publisher. I've met him, he's short of a hundred thousand francs. That'll be a very pleasant way of passing the time. I know nothing about it, but the director is a real Hercules of a man. He'll be in charge, I'll finance things, and everything will go swimmingly. After which I'll get married. And if my wife doesn't please me...

SHE: Yes, my son.

(The conversation tails off.)

3

Tall, thin, beard trimmed to a point, eyes black, neck constricted in a fashionable detachable collar and always dressed with a studied elegance, Mauri de Noirof was the most perfect example of the man-of-the-world. He carried this off by way of his profound urbanity which manifested itself in the minutest details of his life. In the evening, when a *cocotte* of low rank, of very low rank, of really the lowest rank, went *psst, psst* at him, rolling her sunken, come-hither eyes and offering her body for hire by the minute, or the hour, the day, the week or the month; in the evening, when a rosy, chubby-cheeked little boy or an elegant and powdered gentleman brushed against him unequivocally, Mauri would politely excuse himself and bow with exquisite grace to these seekers after love. When he entered a public convenience he removed his hat for as long as he remained there; the act completed, he paid, gave a *sou* or two to the proprietress, never three, and hat in hand, nodded with a smile and left in such a manner as still to seem respectful from behind.

The morning when, for the first time, he climbed the stately staircase to the apartment of the director of the Librairie du Marais, he had something of a shock. He was convinced he had been coming there for some time, that there was nothing new to him in that old Louis XIII house, that he knew the carvings, the panelling, the various peculiarities of the place as well as the inhabitants. He said to the director: "I know you, I've met you before, it's extraordinary, I know your wife as well as your staff; I've always known there'd be a calendar up there, and a sprig of broom in the corner; I can assure you this battered sofa is perfectly familiar to me. Am I mad? Or are you?" The handing-over of the hundred thousand francs and the drawing-up of the partnership agreement had been seen to the day before by the family solicitor. Mauri had a chilly sensation in his head, a chill that froze his brain. He was surprised at the bewilderment of the director, his wife and his staff. A pile of proofs lay on a table; he glanced through them and, although completely ignorant of proofreaders' symbols, removed a superfluous letter with a delete-mark. He got to his feet, discussed how forthcoming publications would fare, then exclaimed: "This is a very easy job, I'll take my leave now, I have other things to see to." The cold feeling in his head intensified. He crossed the Place des Vosges, slapping his cane against his legs and wondering if all the earth's inhabitants were like him. His saliva tasted sweet, he swallowed with pleasure, and the four sides of the ancient royal square faded away behind a shifting yellow veil: there was no longer any sky, the earth was assuming intensely blue tones alternating with others, violet, then green; the leaves on the trees were indigo-tinted, their trunks red, a dazzling red, the air was orange; then suddenly everything was seized with a rapid trembling, and his vision cleared. He collected his thoughts. Then again his head emptied. He stopped thinking, and continued on his way.

He felt something tugging on the sleeve of his frock-coat.

"Don't you recognise me?"

He looked at her curiously.

"But, you know… 34 Boulevard Montrouge… I've come from there for the ballet at the Eden. We're having lunch together, aren't we?"

Not all that pretty. A clear, lush speaking voice. Black hair, too bushy. An impeccable figure. A neat, lascivious, soliciting gait. Nicely shod, clean underclothing, giving off the fragrance of a decent woman. She took his arm and said cheerfully:

"You remember?"

No, he didn't remember. A Valkyrie *leit-motif* was haunting him and, in trying to sing it, he ended up humming a *bal Bullier* waltz. Still unwell? He said:

"I'd dearly like to know, Madame, how it is we're here, at this very spot, at eleven twenty-seven in the morning."

"But you made an appointment with me. The day before yesterday you said: 'Be there.' Here I am. That's it."

"But that's hilarious. I swear the world's full of madmen." Then he added: "… madmen, nothing but loonies. What's your name?"

"Why, La Pondeuse,* of course! You know, if you're embarrassed that I've come along! … You're making out you don't recognise me…"

"La Pondeuse! What a funny name! A *pondeuse* is a woman who must breed something! What do you breed?"

"I don't breed anything. I told you the other day how I got that name."

And she started telling her story over again. As an inveterate gambler, she assiduously attended the races and there risked all her money. For a long time she lived like this on the profits she made at the racecourses, winning five hundred francs today and losing four hundred tomorrow. The balance always in the long run tipped on the profit side. When she appeared at the enclosure, the fanciers and horse-lovers, young and old, exclaimed: "Here's the *ponteuse*; which horse are you going to punt on?" And her punt was almost unerringly correct. One day, out of lazy speaking, they pronounced the word *pondeuse* — and the name stuck. She had a brother, a scoundrel who one night robbed her of everything she possessed, every bit of the ten thousand francs or so she had set aside. Suddenly ruined, she could not bring herself to work and, since she had principles, she enrolled in a brothel. She did not stay there long, barely a week. On the eve of Mauri's apprenticeship at these premises, a magistrate also paid a visit; he was a

33

veteran of the turf, who knew La Pondeuse and forked out for her release.

"So here I am, rescued. This morning I renewed the lease on my Rue Monge apartment. You'll come and visit me, won't you? You'll see just how nice it is. I'll give you chocolate in the morning, Planter's chocolate.* Forain's expression; a bit much, eh?"

He replied: "It's rather annoying they haven't yet found a way of abbreviating the language. Why don't we just pronounce the first syllable of words so as to go quicker? We'll talk about that presently."

"Was I talking about that?"

"Ah yes, the Eden. I remember now. So you're a bit of a dancer? Well, enough of that. I'd like to see a cow in clogs walking a five-hundred-metre-high tightrope between Paris and Marseille."

"I swear he's off his head; he's gaga! You gaga? You drunk?"

And she tickled him amorously under his beard. They hastened on their way, like the heroes of the Flight from Egypt. He said:

"There's nothing so fine as walking fast; every man should have a locomotive in each leg, a tender at his backside, and wheels under his feet."

They skirted the wine market and came to the Rue Cardinal Lemoine where Mauri knew a little restaurant kept by a fat fellow who never smoked. He was known as père La Soupe. The youth of the Latin Quarter did not patronise his establishment because the place was too small. A double door gave access to a sort of antechamber separated from the dining-room by a partition surmounted by balusters, and this partition was pierced by two small windows of frosted glass; these two little windows lent the partition an air of great distinction. The partition had an air of great distinction with its two frosted-glass windows. On entering, one put one's cane and hat, or one's umbrella, or one's parasol in an *ad hoc* wall-cupboard. Then one sat down at a table where no cloth was ever spread;

tables and floor were polished; candles in place of gaslight; an ordinary slate served as a menu — one had to decipher the abridged names of the dishes chalked on it. The food was very good, and value for money; the *patron* waited on the tables himself but refused service when he judged his customers had had enough. The walls were hung, in an artless and wilful disorder, with very bad paintings; cuckoo clocks told the time, and a tame dove flew about from one table to another leaving droppings on the plates. No sooner were they seated than La Pondeuse cried out:

"Why! that's Francisque Sarcey!"*

Père La Soupe was uncommonly like the man. He gave himself airs and graces, and was extremely impolite. He swore he found it distressing to be compared to a literary critic, but in this he was evidently lying since he exhibited a genuine delight at any mention of his double. He spoke rapidly, pronouncing several words all at once, tossing them about in his mouth the way one stirs little fish frying in the pan, and the words would come out haphazardly, one before the other, or simultaneously, or in their proper order. A light flashed on in Mauri's brain, and he leant towards his companion.

"What was I just saying to you?"

"Nothing," she replied, miles away. "This steak is delicious, I could do with another."

"It has to be agreed that a man really is stupid to invite a woman to eat with him. It does nothing at all for the social problem. But see, you're interrupting me; now I don't know what I intended to say."

After a moment's silence:

"Have you a memory? Yes, of course, obviously. So try to repeat everything I've said this morning. I'm not asking for it word for word, the broad outlines of the conversation are enough."

"The broad outlines… That's nice of him with his broad outlines! Ah yes, my dearie, you really can pride yourself on having a screw loose. So, you want the broad outlines. Well now, that cow up in the air, I don't see how that can be called a broad outline."

"In my mind I have glimpses of vast projects that can be carried out. I assure you, I'm afraid of life. Happy people are failures."

"Eat up then, that'll make you feel better."

But he didn't eat. He upset the carafe of water, put pepper in his wine, and was on the point of lighting a cigarette when, in a peremptory tone, La Soupe whispered quietly in his ear: "There's no smoking here, tobacco bothers us." Mauri understood: "'o mokin' 'ere, 'acko 'others us" — and, catching at a fugitive thought, he said to La Pondeuse:

"Listen carefully, this time I've got it. You listening? — 's 'ard t' 'ame a 'ipp. You understand?"

"Not a word."

"That means: it's hard to tame a hippo. It's easily understood. In this way we could abbreviate all words and impress upon conversation a rotary motion which would go very well with a time when everyone is in a hurry being born, living and dying. 'ard t' 'ame a 'ipp…"

"And how are you going to abbreviate this: the sky is no more pure than the depths of my heart?"

"Obviously my system can't always be applied to words of one syllable. Anyhow, I'll be going deeply into the question."

And for two long days he swotted away furiously over the works of de Brosses, B. Tylor and Herbert Spencer;* he went back to the origin of language, to the formation of the first words, studied, or rather tried to study the relation between interjections and the imitative words of different peoples; he was delighted to discover that the Japanese call their mother *caca* and that, in the beginning, man, like the chimpanzee, uttered simple cries to express his emotions. From this he concluded, in a routine sort of way, that the human race was no more than a family of civilised apes.

He rented himself a little fifth-floor apartment on the Rue Campagne-Première. From his study he looked down on to the hackney-carriage depot, a vast edifice with an inner courtyard where, at about five in the morning, all that could be seen was the tops of the fiacres, carefully lined up in ranks. They were tightly packed, almost touching, with their shafts pointing upwards; after cleaning, when they were bunched together for harnessing, from above they looked like huge bedbugs or large, swarming black crabs.

One day Mauri noticed a cabby waving his handkerchief in greeting; the next day, the same routine; with the aid of binoculars Noirof saw it was Pancrace. He liked Pancrace, so he hurried downstairs; at the door of the depot he was almost run over by a railway-station omnibus, then he ventured into the labyrinth of vehicles. The courtyard stank of the urine and dung in which he trod; at first the odour caught at his throat but, once he became accustomed to it, and with a touch of imagination, it came to seem rather exquisite and gave the illusion of a musky patchouli or of a patchoulified musk; or rather that of a *demi-mondaine* worn out by love's tussles and freshly steeped in the multiple scents of the boudoir; or, better still, the illusion of the fragrance of a very respectable woman, celibate, a virgin, jealous and spiteful, smoking Turkish tobacco and sprinkling Eau de Cologne and Lubin in her linen. As soon as Pancrace caught sight of Mauri, he uncrossed his arms and dashed over to him.

"Don't you read the papers? For three days they've been going on about nothing but your disappearance. Apparently you're ruined! What are you up to?"

"Ah my dear fellow, business, business! I'm not doing anything, I'm going through a period of incubation. I'm broody. By the way, though, I've no end of a yen to hire a carriage for a year…"

"Don't you ever do such a thing," the other broke in, in whose spinach-green gaze the ghost of the Dying Tip was already taking form, "hiring a carriage by the year is a swindle. Take me into your service instead; the old rattletrap is decent enough, and so is the nag. I know Paris like the back of my hand, and it's a rare thing for me to have an accident. In all my time I've only squashed six dogs, three women, two men, and four little kiddies at the breast. You'll agree that's not a lot, given the population of the Earth."

Mauri was stroking Pancrace's horse and rolled back its lip to check its age. "What a pity," he said, "one can't see what age women are in this way! You'd only have to make them yawn!"

"Aha! There's a gutsy bugger for you! No flies on him!" exclaimed a cabby harnessing up behind him.

"Fancy a game of dice?"

In the dram-shop on the corner they set the dice a-rolling on the counter. Mauri, who hated wine, paid without drinking himself for endless rounds for the cabbies and ostlers who were poking him in the ribs; there were at least fifteen of them, getting tight on "let's-have-another" of good white, smoking and gesticulating with cheapo stogies, still on the account of the gutsy bugger, as they'd christened Mauri. He himself, up at the crack of dawn, completely bare-chested, was wearing a rosy-cheek-of-a-well-mannered-young-girl-caught-by-a-copper-adjusting-her-garter-in-a-public-place-coloured nightshirt, black velvet trousers and a white morning-coat. Rather at a loss in this unfamiliar company, he clung to the arm of Pancrace, who was gradually getting drunk. At his tenth glass, Pancrace had a bright idea: he suggested they call for an accordionist and then they'd all have a

ball, the lot of them. That would be fun at six in the morning. Everyone agreed. But no musician was to be found. Then, from the huddle of drinkers, a really ugly little man with a twisted mouth emerged, a slap-in-the-gob artist. The inventor of a special sort of music, he could perform excerpts from any opera whatsoever through a series of resounding slaps to his own cheeks. By dint of this battering they had turned puffy and blue on account of the swellings which had not had time to heal; and, when the old fellow treated them to a fearful drubbing, they seemed on the point of falling off. He was a huge success. He played part of *Fleet-foot*, as well as a waltz with the extraordinary title *On the Influence of Air-Currents on the Rotatory Motion of Domestic Fowl*.

Tables and chairs were pushed back against the wall; the musician climbed on to a ladylike little bench, where he had trouble keeping his balance, and which gave him the appearance of a roly-poly toy; the horsewhipping fraternity were shaking a leg, they were not exactly dancing, and raised an astounding hullabaloo with their big boots and clogs and voices made shrill by unforeseen intoxication. All those present were going to a deal of trouble to convince themselves they weren't getting bored. And, since they were starving hungry, they called for breakfast, not much, just some chicken, some cold beef and a bit of cheese. Somebody uttered the word champagne, and Noirof ordered some. He exchanged outfits with Pancrace; in the twinkling of an eye he was transformed into a cabby, and this was such a hit that he felt gurgles of delight inside. Suddenly three women irrupted into the room: La Pondeuse and two of her friends who had been gallivanting all night at Montrouge.* They dragged in behind them an old, dead tomcat, tied to a cord, all stinking, viscous and maggoty. Found in the gutter at three, or rather three-eighteen in the morning. The women were liquored-up and, for a lark, made as if to chuck the cat at somebody's head, a joke enjoyed by all present.

"Let's make it into a stew, it's nice and gamy!"

But the old slap-in-the-gob artist protested — it would be better eaten cold. When they asked him which piece he'd like best, he replied, in a voice as flaccid as his cheeks:

"The unmentionable bit."

And, because they thought he was having them on:

"Really though, the unmentionable bit! That's the best part in animals, and above all in cats, even more so in dead cats, and most of all in worm-eaten dead cats. Oh! To eat that dainty! Or not to eat it…"

It was decided they should toss a coin to see which of the three women should proceed with the ablation of the thing in question: a two-franc piece was tossed in the air and the lot fell to La Pondeuse. But the coin was seen to be a dud, so the matter was again put to the test. Again La Pondeuse was chosen. An enormous and very sharp butcher's knife was brought in on a pewter dish; the rotting carcass was laid on the floor between four burning candles, they formed a circle around it, then champagne glasses were raised and all intoned a pious chant:

> *This is now Mary's month,**
> *Of all the months the fairest.*

La Pondeuse stepped forward, on the one hand with a tear in her eye and, in the other, the blade. There was nothing there to sever. A catricidal knife had eunuchised the poor creature in its tenderest infancy.

"Let me have the tail then, just a bit, a tiny little bit of fifty centimetres, no more than that."

And the roly-poly toy devoured it, even though it was alive with maggots. In a corner a cabby sickened by the scene was puking; his neighbour did likewise, and in less than twenty to twenty-three seconds there was a general vomiting in the dram-shop. The inn reeked with the odour of carcass and undigested drink and all that could be heard was the racket of drunken eructations, the torrents of

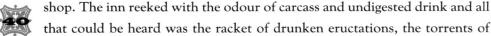

unassimilated liquids, and perfectly involuntary farts. The owner, the owner's wife, the waiter and the waitress were all voiding the contents of their stomachs by their buccal orifices. Alone, still standing on his little bench, the artist revelled in his triumph; slowly he carried on chomping, and as maggots spilled from the corners of his mouth he would deftly catch them up again and munch on them with relish. And when he had finished this diabolical repast, he treated the company to a piece of funeral music, a *de profundis* firmly applied to his cheeks. The cat was removed, there was a moment of calm and they all stared at one another. God! how idiotic they looked!

Somewhat sobered, Pancrace said to Noirof:

"Really though, the papers are full of it. You ought to go and see your mother."

And there and then they started off. Noirof himself drove a fiacre, still dressed as a cabby, the remainder of the band following in fourteen vehicles, scorching along the roadways. When the procession reached the Rue de Presbourg, the neighbourhood was in turmoil, as if expecting a police raid. Madame de Noirof looked out of her window and did not at first recognise her son in the cabby mounting the steps and blowing her kisses. But she was obliged to acknowledge the facts when the door of her room burst open and the fruit of her womb appeared, saturated in all his splendour.

"Oh, my child, how you stink! And that get-up! What's come over you? You haven't shown your face for a month. I've been worried. I went to the police. What have you been getting up to in Valence?"

"In Valence?"

And she showed him a police report referring to his visit to Valence a fortnight previously.

"And with a woman, what's more! And a great fat woman, at that! God! Is it possible? And you so well brought up!"

He protested. The report was untrue. He hadn't left Paris.

"You can ask La Pondeuse, she was right there too. I slept with her for I don't know how many days; then I slept with the big black one from the Marais; then I slept with Gigitte."

And he counted them out on his fingers — he'd bedded eighty-two women, in a month! His mother listened entranced, drinking in his words.

"You must be mistaken, Mauri, just think now, eighty-two women!"

He went over the figures and came to a total of ninety-eight and a half.

"Well then," he said, "give or take fifty-odd, I have it about right."

She took him by the hands, gazed into his eyes, then thrust him away.

"If you're deceiving me, you'd better watch out. I adore you because you're not in the least like other men. You're unbalanced, you don't understand that your nature is superior to that of others. Resembling the common run of men is but an irony of fate. Remember one thing, and that is that life is only a Sensation, and that it ought to be an Extraordinary Sensation. There is no after-life. The soul is no more than the ferment of matter. Off you go, you're troubling me. You make me happy."

And she likewise troubled him; and likewise, she made him happy. Their gazes and their innermost selves coalesced; in the silence of that rococo apartment, cluttered with fake antique furniture and fake modern crockery, one thing alone was genuine: the hidden passion they felt for each other. And when Mauri met up with his escort again it was with good reason that he reflected bitterly that the Divinity itself, notwithstanding its supreme essence, would never be the equal of humanity, since, in his capacity as unacknowledged bastard, God could never permit him to become his mother's lover.

That evening, at the residence of the Duc de la Croix de Berny, there was a celebration. At the bottom of each of the two hundred invitations was written: *The Bishop of Djurdjura will be present. There will be dancing.*

Two or three times a year, the Bishop of Djurdjura, who was most attractive to the ladies, liked to leave behind the inclement climate of Africa and reinvigorate himself with a few minor debauches in Paris. He was the general topic of conversation in society circles on account of his liaison with Madame Perle, a high-flying *cocotte* who was very influential at the Christian court in Rome, and who on various occasions had journeyed there to kiss the Pope's toe to effect the advancement of her pet prelate. It was duly attested in the Vatican that the Holy Father, Brown-Sequarding* though he might be, was very much enfeebled at the end of each of the audiences granted to Madame Perle, and this gossip never failed to stir a flicker of jealousy in the heart of the Bishop of Djurdjura.

"You're deceiving me with Leo XIII!"

"Oh, do be quiet, Monsignor, I'm clearing the way for you to become pope."

The town house of the Duc de la Croix de Berny, on the Boulevard Saint-Germain, was an edifice resembling a theatre, or rather a circus. By way of a long covered entry, sited in a garden, one reached a sumptuous staircase which has been trodden by the feet of an infinity of majesties, lords, queens and women of disrepute. The first floor was made up of a series of rooms which, every year, lost a little of their luxury because their owner, a perpetually unlucky gambler, settled his most pressing debts by giving up some costly paintings or items of furniture to his creditors. At receptions, the resulting gaps were filled with flowers and rare plants borrowed from the State Greenhouses. Above these rooms was a quite enormous auditorium, an exact copy of the one at the Alhambra according to the documents of the city of Granada. Viollet-le-Duc and Garnier* collaborated in secret on the construction of this theatre, one of the most beautiful in the city. It cost the Duc de la Croix de Berny nearly eight million. His friend the King of Bavaria* came in person one day to sample the acoustics and, not being satisfied, the Duc had the ceiling, originally carved, replaced by another in beaten gold. It measured twenty-five metres in diameter, and was supported by four pillars hewn from a single piece of black marble encrusted with gold and garnets. The floor was nothing less than an immense Venetian mirror; when women walked upon it they had no trouble understanding why the men's gaze was constantly lowered: they were trying to investigate their under-clothing. On carved ivory pedestals lined up on each side of the hall stood statues which were removed when festivities took place, and the walls were hung with gold brocade spangled with rubies. There was a salon before the entrance to the theatre; around it ran a continuous plinth which usually supported a motley collection of rare bronzes which were also removed for festivities.

As the Bishop of Djurdjura made his entry, a hidden orchestra struck up the Marseillaise and a riot of electric light flooded over the groups of naked women who had taken the place of the bronzes on the plinths. They were as motionless as marble statues. And from here and there among these white and living bodies there came the sombre note of a live dog or elephant, each on its own plinth and as motionless as the women, and which the Duc had trained especially *for this sort of performance*. This display of human and animal flesh was one of the high spots of the evening; it sent a thrill of wonderment through everyone in the room and made the Bishop giggle with pleasure like a silly little girl. He was tipsy, having drunk more than his fill at dinner with Madame Perle, a dinner which had come to but a trifling eighty thousand francs for the ten guests at table. Ministers, senators, aristocrats both male and female, all in a frisky mood, had responded to the Duc de la Croix de Berny's invitation, and so it was with an uncertain gait that they entered the theatre where, once again, on the carved ivory pedestals, the living statues stood. The Bishop ran his hand over the calves of one of them, a very pretty model from Montparnasse by the name of Philomène. Philomène, who wasn't in the least solemn, was playing the part of Diana the huntress; when she felt the sacerdotal groping of which she was the object she could not restrain an outburst of explosive laughter, and piddled on his lordship's hand. At the same moment, the magnificent Great Dane, on whose head her hand was resting, lifted its tail and dropped a colossal turd. The Bishop blessed these excretions and took his place in the orchestra stalls amid a thunderous round of applause.

The entertainment consisted of a new one-act opera, *The Eyes of Desdemona*. Burgunde, a medieval lord, having heard tell of a very pretty princess who lived a long way, a very long way away in an inaccessible castle, resolves to ride out in order to set eyes upon her. The legend tells that all those who have undertaken this journey have never returned — one single glance from the princess induces in them a fatal shock. But the Devil appears to Burgunde, who gives him half his soul, on condition that Satan swears to return him safe and sound to his domains. The pact is signed in letters of blood on the back of a toad; this blood is drawn from the veins of a ninety-nine-year-old sorceress who has three boils on her left arse-cheek, three boils on her right arse-cheek, a nose the shape of a trowel, feet shaped like fingers, hands shaped like feet and ears the shape of hands. Burgunde sets off, accompanied by the Devil, but is inconvenienced by being only half alive, which he bitterly regrets.

"To see this princess is worth far more than half a life," Beelzebub argues.

"But I am half dead," Burgunde responds, "and the prospect of so cock-eyed an existence is not at all attractive."

They arrive at the princess's castle. The nobleman looks at her, and recognises his wife, a fearful shrew who left him to embark upon a series of adventures, each one more amorous than the last, and who immediately cuckolds him with his infernal companion. Burgunde returns home, utterly crestfallen, encounters the toad, crushes it underfoot, and dies.

A society lady, a very talented musician, had improvised a very poor accompaniment to this baroque libretto, and the verses, from the pen of one of our most famous Academicians, were yet more mediocre; the entire interest, however, resided in the ballet, performed by stark-naked dancing-girls. The Duc himself directed it, and had reserved for himself the role of the principal dancer, which he carried off rather lamely. He made his entrance in a red costume with a tutu and a yellow tarlatan skirt spangled with real roses; he blew kisses in all directions, and smiled like a man constipated. The audience found his performance thoroughly inferior, and applauded frenetically.

Mauri de Noirof said to his mother:

"She's very nice, that little miss there. She looked shocked throughout the performance. She's a well-brought-up young person."

"Would you like me to introduce you?"

"I'd be delighted."

Her name was Hermine Israël. The Noirofs and the Israëls were acquainted because for a long time they had been bumping into each other regularly at an antique-dealer's on the Rue Férou. Hermine was twenty-eight. A very chubby girl,

 neither beautiful nor pretty, a rosy complexion, brunette, with sensual lips and eyes as gentle as a lamb's. Her late father had been one of the leading dealers in pawn-tickets at the Paris Mont-de-Piété, and she lived with her mother in a little mezzanine flat on the Boulevard Saint-Germain. The Israëls survived on a private income of a hundred thousand francs.

"And, on top of that, the girl is due to inherit two or three hundred thousand francs from an elderly aunt," Madame de Noirof added when the others' backs were turned.

"Is she at least still a virgin?"

"Ah! You'll understand that I haven't poked my nose into that! In any case virginity is of no importance in a rich young girl."

"That was a very stupid question I put to you anyhow: she still has it; I saw that in the vagueness of her gaze and the cloying tone of her voice. When a young girl looks and speaks poorly like that, she's still a virgin."

The crowd was slowly dispersing and spilling out through the rooms on the first floor. There remained only a few very elderly, very decorated gentlemen, lingering among the statues. The Bishop approached Mauri's mother.

"So, Madame, I take it I may put you down for two hundred thousand francs? Excellent. Since your son's an engineer, he can come and see the gold mine."

Hermine was thinking:

"He's very distinguished, that young man, but he ogles his own mother!"

And Mauri had become thoughtful. Leaning against a wall in the corner of the salon, he was musing upon human stupidity and the universal law of hypocrisy. Every one of the Duc de la Croix de Berny's guests appeared content with themselves, but that wasn't so. A truly happy man is one whose brain has been emptied, whose legs, hands and ears have been cut off, his eyes put out and his sense of taste destroyed. He no longer senses, no longer thinks, he is animalised, he is out of this world. Select a human animal, no matter which; upon closely examining it, one is certain to find at least one imperfection, and that imperfection is the exhalation, the product, the fermentation of a decomposing consciousness. A smile is always hideous because it is only the mask of an imperfection. Mauri was suffering, he felt hammer-blows in his head and the proximity of his fellows made him ill at ease; he had a horror of crowds, the human plasma irritated his nerves; he was about to leave when Madame Perle came over and shook him by the arm.

"Well now, young man, having a good time, eh? Have you had a smoke yet by any chance? You know we always have a dance on Saturdays at my at-homes, but it's dull when you're not there. You understand?"

"I'll be there on Saturday, Madame. By the way, tell me, would you, what was that two hundred thousand francs the Bishop was talking about just now?"

"Ah yes, for the foundation of the basilica at Montmartre."*

The reply astonished de Noirof. Two hundred thousand francs for the foundation of a church! His mother was going out of her mind, she'd be stony broke in no time. The railway accident had brought in four hundred thousand francs, but there couldn't be much left.

"There's nothing left," she said when they emerged. "I've heard nothing from the man with the camel nose, he's swindled me out of fifty thousand francs. And how's your book business?"

"Business? My word, you're right! I'd clean forgotten that thingummy. I'll go there tomorrow. I'll tie a knot in my hanky to remind me. I suppose it's still carrying on. But for the love of that old bitch of a supreme being that goes by the name of God and who spends his time getting up to monkey-business with the women who go to heaven, how are you going to live?"

"By marrying you off, my dear. You shall marry Hermine, and that way we'll be living in clover."

"Living in clover! That's easily said, but all the same there's no need to go tossing the odd two hundred thousand francs into all the basilicas of

France and Navarre!"

"There isn't any basilica, Madame Perle got mixed up. The Bishop of Djurdjura is setting up a colossal business-deal, to open up the silver mines at Monte Rubio. He needed three million, he's just got four. He's giving the surplus to the basilica at Montmartre. He's a very powerful man, he'll be pope one of these days. We have everything to gain by being nice to him."

The next day Mauri rang the bell for the manager of the Librairie du Marais. The door remained shut. His partner in business had scarpered, neglecting to leave his new address.

Mauri had better luck with the Israëls. Mademoiselle Hermine's mother welcomed him with open arms.

"She's not in, but she'll be back. You've met before, haven't you? She's a charming young thing."

She showed him some embroidery executed by the young lady's fair hands.

"She's as industrious as ever two could be, never mind one. Would you like me to show you the family portraits?"

And she led him into a drawing-room tightly packed with paintings which she enumerated with a catch in her voice. There were masses of Jewish portraits, of uncles, grandfathers, great-grandfathers' dogs, brothers-in-law's horses, nieces' cats. Then she heaved a deep and emotional sigh as she halted before a huge oval canvas:

"That's my daughter's portrait. Her brandy's there in front of her."

"Her brandy?"

"Yes, that's what it was. When Hermine was sitting for it she was suffering from a touch of toothache, and in order to ease the pain she would wash out her mouth with cognac. The artist missed nothing. For a whole week he ruined his eyes to reproduce the cotton threads of the young girl's coloured dress.

"See for yourself — there are threads in red, blue, green and white. The reds and the greens are vertical, the others are horizontal. The green goes under the blue and over the white; the white goes under the green and over the red. The resemblance is quite striking. And the likeness, eh? It's there!"

"Yes, but it lacks a certain dewiness."

"You think so?"

Hermine came in. She too thought it lacked a certain dewiness. And the word suggested to her the idea of having a drink.

Mauri was inspecting his future wife. God, how fat she was! Never could he bring himself to make her his better half, he who wished only for the happy medium! That such a woman should occupy a place in a man's life! Snuggled up in her armchair, she was poking mechanically with a podgy finger in her nose and extracting filaments of snot which she kneaded into tiny pellets. She then ate these pellets. Mauri counted seventeen she swallowed thus, one after another, in this charming manner. A methodical woman, to be sure, who let nothing go to waste. And she took her drink neat, pouring brimful glasses of kümmel and chartreuse because she was still feeling a slight tingling sensation in a right upper molar, or rather a lower one, she was no longer quite sure which; it was, though, on the right side. She told them she'd been to her milliner for an alteration, then to her umbrella-dealer to have the handle of her brolly-cum-sunshade changed. Her manner of speaking was rather whiny and peevish. Frequently, when she paused for breath, she would stick her tongue out like a little girl reciting a catechism lesson.

The marriage was fixed for the beginning of October. Hermine would be bringing a dowry of seven hundred thousand francs in bank-notes; Mauri would be bringing nothing, but his mother would furnish his apartment and they would be trying, in the meanwhile, *to find something for him.* Furthermore, he would have to go and make sure the Monte Rubio silver deposits really existed. That in any case would keep him occupied.

5

A new crisis befell him.

One day he had a clear vision of a mountain of living carp from the summit of which he was dispensing his blessings to a multitude of crocodiles fed on human beings. This was the realisation of a macabre vow: his association with God, with the aim of exterminating, by means of an electrically assimilable poison, all the inhabitants of Earth. He alone would survive the general extinction, thereby revelling in the unique delight of every man professing a profound disgust for his fellows: to be the Last One to die.

So he went to see God. The latter was having a foot-bath when Mauri rapped on the door of paradise.

"Come in!" a voice called out.

He pushed open an invisible door and fell into the arms of a very young man who said:

"I was expecting you, my good fellow, I know why you're here. We're going to sort them out."

"Are you God?" Mauri asked.

"Of course," the other replied. "It surprises you, doesn't it, not seeing me as the wizened old dotard they like to show in those third-rate engravings in all your missals and books of hours? That's how it is... that's how it is; I rejuvenate myself when the fancy takes me. You don't mind, do you, if I get rid of this shit that's cast a pall on my right big toe? With you in a minute… Ah, my dear fellow, what a high old time I just had with the seraphines! A party that lasted seven hundred years! What a booze-up! You've no idea what it's like, you lot, living down there like civvies. And when you do get round to knocking it back, just for a night, you wake up with a thick head in the morning."

After a moment of silence:

"This heaven of mine, old fellow, is a thorough bloody mess, I'm really disappointed, it's worse than Bordenave's plays; in the old days the Virgins were always grovelling at my feet, now they don't give a toss about me, they have a bit on the side. There's some who don't even want to go to bed with me any more, they prefer oldsters like that swine Saint Peter and that rotter of a Jesus Christ. There's another one that's gone to the bad, that Jesus Christ. He's not ageing at all well; he's an ingrate. In the name of Me, I swear I'll boot him out one of these days."

He groused and grumbled on for a few minutes more; then, when he'd finished paring his toenails, he took Mauri by the arm.

"I'm going to show you something very odd — a collection of souls."

From space he detached a panel which might have measured some five or six thousands of millions of myriametres square, entirely besmirched with tiny, black, very unsightly spots.

"You see, they all look the same. That's rather amusing! The whole lot will roast in hell one day! I've seven or eight hundred million similar panels, completely filled with damned souls. See how everything is in order; later on there will be no possibility of confusion."

He handed Mauri a moderately powerful spyglass and had him look at the Earth: it resembled a dunghill heaving with vermin, a bolus of corruption.

"I made a serious mistake in creating your planet. It's giving me more trouble than the rest of the Finite Universe. Ah, you lot haven't been at all smart, you've steered your ship badly. Your civilisation is stupid. I let you get on with it because that amuses me, but just see how conceited you are! You know perfectly well that a multiplicity of laws is one of the obvious signs of a people's decadence, and yet your politicians create new ones daily. And such disagreements between your legal systems! If I had populated the moon, its inhabitants wouldn't have been as cuntish as you lot. The human race disgusts me because it's gone too flaccid too soon."

"So where is hell then?" Mauri asked.

"Down there, to the left, about two quintillion leagues away; like to see it?"

"Yes please. And purgatory?"

"Ah, that's an invention of your Holy Mother Church. I can tell *you* that as soon you'll be the only one of your race left alive. You know I'm enormously indebted to you, yes, to you. I was about to get myself involved in a stupid affair. I'd promised the sister of Jesus Christ I'd have a bit of fun with her for ten thousand years. (I must admit Jesus Christ's sister comes of a good family, a bit thick, but with possibilities.) She came over to my place, we had a little drink together, and she persuaded me, the scheming bitch, to be her pimp for a period of two thousand lustra,* and at that moment I heard you say to your mother, as you left the Duc de la Croix de Berny's ball, that I was getting up to some hanky-panky with the women of Heaven. You know, that stopped me short! I don't like people telling the truth about me."

A teardrop, a thousand times more copious than the Ocean, trickled from his left eye; another teardrop, ten thousand times more copious than the Ocean, trickled from his right eye; a sigh, as thunderous as a simultaneous salvo of nine hundred and ninety-nine thousand million cannon, convulsed his breast. He said to Mauri:

"You have led me back into the way of virtue, you have vexed me; the rest of humankind must pay the price."

At that moment everybody was eating. With an adroitness as remarkable as that of an adolescent plunging a dagger into the heart of his dearly beloved sister, God deposited in their victuals an electric spark overloaded with prussic acid, and, instantaneously… Heaven was invaded by a cloud of exceedingly black souls. Crocodiles loomed up on all sides and devoured the corpses, and it was from the summit of a mountain of living carp that Mauri enjoyed this truly grandiose spectacle. A purple veil hung in space, streaked with mica flakes of unsullied consciences; the four corners of the veil were upheld by naked, transparent angels, and while the Earth disintegrated, the divine orchestra played this triumphal march:

THE TWILIGHT OF THE FLESH

Music by GOD   Lyric by THE WORD

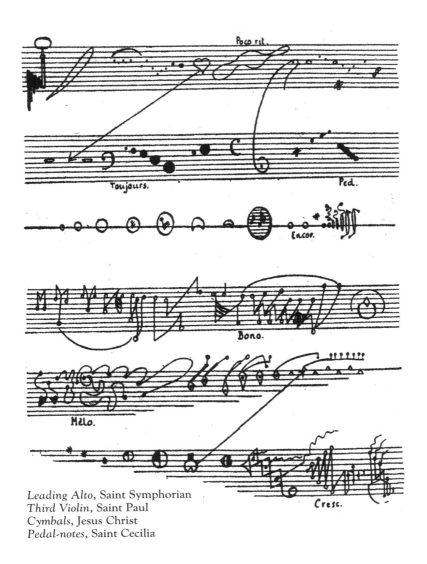

Leading Alto, Saint Symphorian
Third Violin, Saint Paul
Cymbals, Jesus Christ
Pedal-notes, Saint Cecilia

When Mauri awoke, his surprise at finding himself to be incorporeal was considerable, and it was only after a painful inner struggle that he succeeded in establishing who he was. The train was travelling at full speed; where was it taking him? It must be Spain, to investigate the silver deposits. He could not remember any more. He could not understand what he was doing. He patted himself down, and groaned to find his body ached all over. Everything astonished him, the carriage he was in, the night, the stars, the noise and juddering of the train. He pondered: everything seemed new to him, even his hands, his legs, his feet. He asked himself: where am I from? who am I? where am I going? but he could not answer these questions. A strange process was taking place within him; the dryness of his throat was making him yawn, and a superabundance of vigour was threatening to make him explode into fragments. A very vague self-awareness convinced him he was enormously different from his fellow men.

A setback awaited him at Monte Rubio — the trail of the silver deposits had petered out; in point of fact, the Bishop of Djurdjura, in cahoots with some shifty character of a Spanish politician, had siphoned off a few millions from the Duc de La Croix de Berny's entourage in order, with the latter's agreement, to set up some *maisons de tolérance** for the use of ecclesiastics in Paris. Mauri returned home, happy at the collapse of his mother's fortune. Certain sorrowful events can fill us with joy. Madame de Noirof heard the news with a vivid astonishment mitigated by admiration. She said to her son:

"That's it then, what can one do? Perhaps one day we'll be luckier."

Mauri paid his court to Mademoiselle Hermine quite mechanically. He would arrive at the Boulevard Saint-Germain in a splendid brougham, driven by Pancrace; every time he would bring flowers and would find the young girl at table,

 between a small bottle of liqueur and a box of cigarettes; she drank and smoked in order to strengthen her gums; each time the young man found her more and more dumpy, it seemed to him she was growing smaller by degrees, gaining in plumpness and losing in height. She weighed herself frequently, and ascertained that the action of gravity bore down upon her body ever more heavily from one day to the next. She was always careful to visit the W.C. before using the scales, in order to get a more accurate measurement of her weight.

The contrary was happening with de Noirof — he was becoming taller and thinner. An itch to be on the move tormented him, and he could not keep still. Walking was repulsive to him; he abominated those who didn't go gadding about in cabs. As an entirely logical consequence, there was a place reserved in his heart for horses and cabbies. He favoured trains too; and the idea that one day one might succeed in going round the world in a second left him starry-eyed. Since his memory was defective he would scribble no end of things in a little notebook. One day he wrote down the word *pneumatic*.

He had been called upon to find the apartment he was to occupy with his young wife, once the honeymoon was over. Mauri decided upon one on the sixth floor in the Rue de Rennes. Hermine protested: "The sixth!" Was there at least a lift? There wasn't.

"My daughter is a charming young person, but she's lazy; to climb up to the sixth floor, for her, is quite an ordeal. And to think it's all been settled! All the same... a bit high up... don't you think?"

"Not at all. Me, I just love climbing stairs. Besides, nobody will be forcing Hermine to go downstairs or upstairs any more than she wants to."

And he added a quip in poor taste:

"When she can't any more, why then she'll come to a full stop."

A discussion then arose on the subject of furniture. Mauri wanted Italian, Hermine wanted Breton.

"Oh!" she exclaimed, "those Breton tables from Landivisiau and Saint-

Thégonnec, those carved rustic cupboards from Pont-Aven and the Pont-Aven box-beds, you're so comfy in them. Wouldn't you like to sleep in a Pont-Aven box-bed?"

She gazed at him with her big, beautiful eyes, all overflowing with goodness, which pierced deep into his inmost self.

"A box-bed? To suffocate in? Thanks very much! Ah, Italian furniture, that's the only sort. It's stylish, it's light, it's all skies and sunlight."

But he realised that the inclinations of this fat little woman were wholly directed towards ugly and massive objects. Furthermore, Madame Israël raised an objection to which he was obliged to submit:

"Blue skies and sunlight, that's not very solid. Can you see Hermine sitting in a chair made of blue skies and sunlight? The chair would break in no time, my daughter would fall and do herself an injury. Suppose she fell on an eight-inch nail that pierced her in the flesh of her backside, what a business that'd be!"

So they purchased a suite of Breton furniture. Mauri de Noirof took a secret pleasure in selecting the most tasteless, the most cumbersome, the squattest and the dreariest; he set his heart upon rustic pieces, the most down-to-earth, the most rugged, put together by rural carpenters and upon which a clumsiness of workmanship, and coarseness and naïveté of conception imprinted a seal of frozen hideousness.

Fearing that Hermine might be gifted with second sight, the young man consulted one of the *princes of medical science*. He became convinced he would remain slim for as long as he lived. His future wife's soul was not therefore closed to aesthetic matters, since she wanted a husband of middling build.

Now and then she would ask him:

"Do you like this? Do you like that?"

Their preferences always ran counter to one another. This difference left

Mauri quite dazed. He adored spicy foods, she loathed pepper and mustard. Confectionery and alcohol — which she relished with spasms of delight — gave him, for his part, stomach trouble. And when, delicately, he brought up the subject of the carnal pleasures marriage authorised between persons of a different sex, she gave him to understand that she would never like *that*, that *that* wasn't nice, that she didn't get married for *that*, that she was as frosty as the machine in the morgue.

"I've already tried," she said. "I never could again."

"Could what?"

She lowered her eyes, did not blush but replied, still in a muffled tone:

"Well, *that*!"

"Who with?"

"Oh, with my moral tutor. The more I think about *that*, the more deathly rigid I become, the more I encoffin my senses *ad hoc*. Listen now, if we go on talking about *that*, I'll catch cold."

She'll catch cold! He thought he was dreaming. Was she too off her head? That was splendid then!

She asked him:

"Will you be faithful to me?"

"Not in the least, my dear, not in the least little bit."

"Nor me neither; I have a feeling I'll have moments of sinful abandon. I shall deceive you with myself. In such cases the law is easy on adulteresses!"

In his little notebook Mauri wrote down the word *guillotine*. Then he interrupted his courtship for a month.

For a month he was in the grip of a passion for a monstrosity being exhibited at the Hippodrome:* it was a woman with two heads, four legs and four arms; she had a single pelvis and just one stomach; they called her Mani-Mina. Born in the Tyrol, she had toured all the towns of Germany, Switzerland and

Belgium, and had just made her début in Paris playing the violin on her right side and the clarinet on her left. She performed a duet, solo; the right was soprano, the left contralto. She gave the lie to the proverb that holds one cannot do two things at once. Mauri fell for the right side; this paid off nicely because, one evening, after a very successful performance, he waited for the double woman at the exit and invited her to supper. Mani accepted, Mina pulled a face, but had to resign herself to it. They went to Chez Maire.* They ate and drank for six, with the result that they left the restaurant in somewhat high spirits. The prospect of a night of love unique of its kind tickled Mauri's fancy deliciously; he made improper suggestions; one said yes, the other said no.

"I don't want to," said Mina.

"But I do," the other responded. "Why do you say no? It has to happen to all of us one day." Speaking to Noirof, she continued: "You know, it's the first time…"

Mani-Mina was taken to a cheap hotel in the quartier du Temple, a hotel that reeked of cut-price streetwalkers. She got twenty-five francs for the evening, though that seemed scarcely enough.

"You know, twenty-five francs for two, that's only twelve-fifty each. We hardly make two ends meet, and until now there has been no lover to initiate us into carnal delights, nobody has helped us out. There again, if Mina weren't unwell! But there you go, she is."

Mina did indeed have a little sore on her right thigh, a red patch around a suppurating pustule. Other little red spots were scattered almost everywhere over her wretched skeleton of a body, a body as gnarled as a box-tree root.

"Oh! I know full well I'm done for!"

A shudder of horror ran through the other one: it was the first time the idea that their life could come to an end had been expressed by her sister.

When this freak of nature was undressed, Mauri had a moment of hesitation. Should he bed it? This strange body, joined below the waist, had only one spinal column: naked it resembled two flayed calves, back to back on a butcher's slab. The skin was pale — apart from Mina's, which was mottled with red blotches. Two very distinct odours issued from the body, an odour of decay, and one of fresh meat, an odour of life and one of death. The mixture was nauseating. To possess such a being bordered on desecration, but the unexpected attraction overcame Noirof's scruples; however, he had an atrocious night. He lost his way among the multitude of limbs, some of which embraced him while others fought him off; he got confused, warmly embraced Mina, and when Mani protested he lost his head and wanted, for certainty's sake, to put the two sister's heads together, but the spinal column balked at this and the body slackened like an unstrung bow. The Lord's little game left him feeling it had all been a nightmare. Besides, Mina-Mani's skin was as sticky as that of an octopus. That, doubtless, was why he found it so difficult to break free.

He remained there, in fact, glued to them for a month, to the great delight of the patrons of the Hippodrome. An ironic paragraph in a morning paper, making fun of him, made him determined to come unstuck. He returned to the Rue Campagne-Première where he found letters and telegrams from Madame Israël and his mother: they were asking whether or not he wished to get married.

"My head! My poor head," he cried out in desperation.

And he forgot everything, his trip to Monte Rubio, his flirtation with Mani-Mina. He was surprised at the reproaches being laid against him.

"Very well then, marry us as soon as may be; let's make an end of it."

But he wanted it done post-haste.

"You gave us a fright," Madame Noirof told him. "Just think of how I'm ruined! How do you expect me to live? As it happens I made an excuse for your twenty-eight days' absence and talked your future mother-in-law into doubling the dowry. Ah, you can be pleased at how much your mother loves you."

The marriage was solemnised in Saint-Germain-des-Prés. The bride, the groom and the wedding guests were all in mourning. They had decided on this so as *not to do what everybody else does.* The Bishop of Djurdjura delivered a ribald allocution; he discoursed at length on the pleasures of marriage and, with his voice lowered, added a hint: "You'll have a high old time of it, my dears, and France'll be grateful to you for it one of these days."

An ill-assorted procession was assembled in the sacristy: the Duc de la Croix de Berny, Madame Perle, Pancrace, along with all the cabbies from the Montparnasse depot, La Pondeuse, Jardisse and the cheek-slapping artist who had eaten the dead cat. It was raining in torrents, and it was cold. And it was with an unutterable uneasiness that each one of them left the church.

"Godard! Where's Godard? Anybody seen Godard?"

Mauri searched the nooks and crannies of the Place Saint-Germain-des-Prés: no trace of Godard.

"Ah well, to La Villette!"*

To La Villette! Nobody understood why. They were supposed to be dining at Magny's,* then letting the young people make off for the Midi.

They argued in the rain, and, so as to please everybody, it was decided that half should go to Magny's and the other half to La Villette.

"What are we supposed to do in La Villette?"

"You'll see," said Mauri. "It's quite amazing."

Sitting next to his wife, he took out of his pocket a compass, a thermometer and a frog.

"Tools of the trade," he said. "All will become clear."

"Why don't you speak nicely to me, Mauri?"

"What for? There'll be plenty of time for stupidities."

"Are you happy?"

"Not in the least. I'm yawning. I detest the human race."

"Me too."

And she stroked the frog, a little green frog afflicted with big eyes like those of an ophicleide-player whose instrument is blocked and who is blowing with all his might into the mouthpiece so that his fellows don't feel fucked off with him. The frog's eyes resembled those eyes, but only of course to a certain extent, say, one to nine-and-a-half.

"It really is most interesting," she added, "for a young bride to be going with her husband to La Villette in the rain, cheek-to-cheek with a frog."

"I take your word for it," he replied. "It doesn't happen to every woman."

And the taste of the cigar he had smoked, long ago, at Madame Perle's returned to his mouth. Then, closing his eyes, he saw again the Duc de la Croix de Berny in his dancing-girl costume. And he dozed off. She woke him at La Villette.

Godard* was there, waiting for him.

"We have very nasty weather, but I've brought lots of ballast and we'll soon be through the clouds…"

A balloon was moored in the yard of the gas-works. It was equipped with two nacelles, one above the other, the upper one much larger than the lower.

"You understand now?" Mauri asked Hermine. "Usually, when one gets married, one is full of joy and takes the P.L.M.* to go and perfom the nuptial gymnastics in the worn-out and bug-infested beds of provincial inns. Well now, we're not going to copy anybody, we'll do things another way entirely and spend our first night married three thousand metres above the ground. We're going to climb into the top nacelle; it's upholstered and has everything necessary for you know what. Don't forget the frog."

63

And, with the swiftness of an acrobat, without bidding farewell to anyone, he leapt into the conjugal basket. But Hermine wouldn't hear of such a voyage.

"Then I'll go on my own; *you can stay at home*. But if I run into some other woman, that's your hard luck."

This last argument decided his wife. With the utmost difficulty, she hoisted herself up next to him. The balloon descended a little under the weight of this anti-Lilliputian creature. They had to jettison some ballast in order to regain their equilibrium.

Slowly, and without majesty, the aerostat at length rose into the air.

6

"Yes my dear, that's how it is. I'm smitten with you, even more so since I saw you out on foot, followed by a maidservant. Just think, you, on foot! And with a skivvy in tow! You really are a card. How wrong you were, getting married!"

She was showing him round her little place on the Rue Monge, an ante-room, a living-room, a bedroom, with kitchen and all modern conveniences. The whole was very comfortably furnished, without ostentation, however, a mere superfluity of choreographic emblems blemished the southwest end of the living-room. But because of the dimness of the lighting, Mauri was hard put to make out very much. On top of that, his mind was on other things. He was eager to go to bed.

"Even so, it is rather funny," La Pondeuse said, "that you're not spending your first night as a married man with your wife! What's so odd about her?… Won't she…? Doesn't she have any…?"

"You'll read all about it in the papers tomorrow."

"We'll get up at midday, because I have to go to the rehearsal of *Le Cœur de Sita*. I was lucky enough to get into the Eden. Yesterday I lost two hundred francs at the races. I haven't a thing left to put on my feet; I ordered a pair of Molière slippers, they'll be bringing them round tomorrow but I'm stony broke. Really, it's too bad, I'll send them back!"

La Pondeuse was devoted to her pets; she had a cat, a dog, a little guinea-pig, and these quadrupeds gambolled about on the quilt letting out their grunts, yaps and mews of delight. Mauri, who detested people, was hardly more enthusiastic about animals, and it was with a frown that he tumbled into bed. Something chilly wrapped itself around his legs: it was a grass snake, two grass snakes, three grass snakes, completely inoffensive to be sure, along with a lizard, likewise inoffensive, whose slumber he was disturbing.

"Don't be afraid, my dear, they're harmless. The grass snakes know me, I brought them up. I'm going to suckle them, you'll see, it's frightfully amusing."

And after a silence:

"Oh, the trouble they are! I'm always cleaning up after them, it's such a bore!"

She picked up one of the grass snakes and, uncovering a breast, she thrust the nipple into its mouth. In less than five minutes, bloated with milk, the creature could no longer stand up.

"You've had children, then, since you can suckle these ovovivipares?"

"Not at all. I had some special treatment from a famous doctor in Bel-Air. Using his method, all women, even sterile ones, can produce milk. If you like we can go and see him one day, his discoveries are astounding. Tell me now, why aren't you sleeping with your wife tonight?"

"You don't understand why? It's really simple; we've fallen out over a frog she forgot about in the balloon-basket. When we were at an altitude of two thousand, two hundred and thirty-four metres, fifty-six and a half centimetres. She was rude to me; so to avoid any trouble I asked Godard to open the valve and I descended at the very spot we'd set off from. Then she ascended again with Godard. And here I am. Just that, nothing underhand about it. On my journey on the ground I met a canny little maidservant whom I hired on the spot and who carried my bundle home. And that is how the sun of my presence shines this evening in these parts."

 "But you'll patch things up with her when she comes back to you? And the very idea of leaving your wife up in the air with Godard! You know, don't you, that Godard is quite the lecher? And there was nobody to see what they got up to up there."

Another grass snake was suckling in its turn. At every gulp its belly undulated, and its eyes closed in bliss. This one was enormous, and was the size of a slim woman's thigh when it was sated. But La Pondeuse was exhausted and had to postpone until the next day the suckling of the third ophidian, which hissed with annoyance and hunger.

It was an exquisite night for Mauri. He couldn't sleep a wink — the animals indulged in countless capers across his belly-button; the cat nibbled his beard, the dog played hide-and-seek with the guinea-pig in his armpits and the lizard raced up and down his calves. As for herself, she snored like a blacksmith's bellows, and he suffered frequent nightmares. She cried out: "On stage, ladies!… A best rumpsteak for table number one!… Long live the Emperor!…" while in adjoining rooms, creaking bedsteads attested to amorous tussles being endlessly renewed.

In the morning there was a knock on the door: it was the bootmaker with mademoiselle's footwear. La Pondeuse welcomed him into the bedroom.

"You'll have to keep them, I haven't a *sou*, unless he wants to give them to me."

And, turning to Mauri:

"You would like to, wouldn't you, eh? They're fifty francs. Look how pretty they are!"

The bootmaker approached, and sure enough, he was the Israëls' family bootmaker, and it was from him that Mauri had ordered Hermine's wedding slippers. Noirof blushed scarlet.

"Don't you worry at all, Monsieur de Noirof, I know what's what, I won't say a thing."

And seeing the young man's embarrassment he made as if to withdraw, but La Pondeuse retained him; they'd have a glass of Madeira together. A neighbour came in, Mademoiselle Jeanne, a colleague of the boards. And they all drank cheerily. Mauri was still in bed. A charwoman came next, with a bowl of chocolate.

"A Planter's chocolate, my dear? But it's hardly the right moment…"

Nevertheless, he drank it all down, while the rest indulged in another round of Madeira. Mauri would gladly have been miles away; the room was slowly filling up with women who'd come to admire the pair of shoes and eye up the muggins; two tarts from the same landing and a piano-teacher had come in, along with some dogs and cats, and they all chaffed at Mauri, who felt his brow breaking out in a sweat.

They drank steadily. The bootmaker suggested a game of manille, and they seated themselves around a table which they drew up to the bed so that Mauri could follow the play. La Pondeuse was partnered by one of the tarts, and the bootmaker by the piano-teacher. The others looked on. The stake was a bottle of fine Malaga, 44 proof. The tart turned up the ace of diamonds.

"Four points for us."

The bootmaker had a wretched hand: the ten of clubs, unguarded, and two trump-cards, the jack and the queen. His partner was no better off: only the seven, and no ten.

"You're not trumping?"

"Next time, for sure."

"How are you off for clubs?"

"Three."

"A three and a four. That's a strong-'un!"

He slapped down his ten, but La Pondeuse trumped it.

"So, no club then. Are you really with us?"

"The ace, the king and the nine."

"I've got the ten and the eight. I'm trumping with the ten so as to follow up afterwards with a winning hand. Unless I first play my ten of hearts and spades. You got an ace?"

"Clubs? Of course, and the king and the jack."

"That's thirty-four! Hold on while I play my tens. Spades! … Hearts! … The ace of hearts! … Ah! So much for the king, I'm playing the other two, I had all four of them. Hearts! … Hearts! …"

"Hang on to the ace of spades," the bootmaker yelled.

But the tart still had three trumps. A proper thirty-four right there.

With the second deal the bootmaker turned up the king of hearts.

"Ah, shit!" La Pondeuse exclaimed. "I've got nothing. The cards weren't shuffled. How many spades?"

"The eight and the jack."

She played the seven.

"I've got the king and the nine," said the bootmaker. "The ace is with La Pondeuse. Got to cover yourself!"

The piano-teacher came up with her queen, and her partner took the king; then she played the nine again.

"Shit!" La Pondeuse repeated. "The buggers! They've got seventeen straight off!"

"A little club for me now."

The tart had the queen and the ten.

"Some bloody cover!"

But the bootmaker had the unguarded king. And he took the trick.

"Trumps!"

"Are you really with us?" La Pondeuse enquired.

"The jack and the queen."

"I only have the ace. If the pianist lady has the ten she's backing me up."

And sure enough she backed him up.

"Trumps again," bawled the bootmaker, "we're taking her queen. You got the ten of diamonds?"

"Yes, and the ace too. And I've still got the ace of clubs."

"We've thirty-four," cried La Pondeuse. "You needn't have been so defensive with the clubs! It's my fault, I had three, you ought to have held on to your ten."

That left them with thirty-seven points to thirty-eight.

The third hand changed nothing. They had just as many points on one side as on the other.

And Mauri was still in bed. Deafened by the players' exclamations, he dared not rise because his clothes were hanging on the wall on the other side of the table. When he closed his eyes, a succession of scenes played out on the insides of his eyelids: an ivy-hung wall, a straggle of ants climbing up and down a lighted candle, then nothing, a black curtain, then a deserted village on fire, a torrent of naked women with plenty of money in their pockets, a river of pebbles swarming with fish.

"Have you any tens? ... Are you really with us? ... Aren't you trumping?"

Each hand started with these same questions. Now they were playing for another bottle of Malaga, a matter of giving the losers a return match. Only they had to be quick about it because the ladies of the Eden ballet had to take breakfast at ten, and it was already nine thirty-four.

"But you're all right there in beddie-byes, duckies, so you stay there; I bet your wife's having herself a long lie-in too. Just imagine, this lovely man got married yesterday morning, and here he is in my bed!"

Those who were not playing cards gathered round and asked for details. One of them had read about it in the morning's *Petit Journal*. Mauri was oblivious.

"What, you don't know about it?"

"Absolutely nothing, I don't know what you're talking about."

He scanned the article, in which his name was designated only with an X. It said that the balloon had landed at Fleurines, near Senlis, in the grounds of the Château de Saint-Christophe, that Madame X had fainted, and that her first words, on regaining consciousness, had been to ask for a drink. Mauri read all this disinterestedly, and felt entirely uninvolved in the matter.

"But come on now, that's your wife; are you sick or something?"

"I promise you, you're every one of you all at sea. I never was married. I'm beginning to live; I've no idea how old I am. And if I am old, then I've been here a long time, lying in this bed which I'm seeing for the first time."

He looked about him; with each blink of his eyes the objects about him seemed newer and newer. He no longer recognised La Pondeuse. He could not recognise himself any more.

"All the same I'd dearly love to know who I am."

He picked up the paper again: he could no longer read.

"Teach me the alphabet!"

And he added:

"What for though, since all that stuff is pointless. But I'd really like to know what you need to do to live."

His peculiar turn was taking hold now. Bouts of amnesia gripped him during which he uttered complete absurdities. This went on for ten minutes, and then he came to himself again. And he forgot everything that had happened during the attack.

The dancing-girls had lost the second bottle of Malaga. They had time left only to eat and then digest at their leisure, to smoke a pipe, and then make tracks to the Eden.

"I'm not really in good form," La Pondeuse commented, "I rather fancy rehearsing here, how about you, Jeanne?"

"I'm game; only don't be surprised if our pay gets cut!"

"Mauri will make it up for us, won't you dearie? What's she want then, that one over there? Ah, of course, she didn't have her drinkie yesterday."

And she suckled the third grass snake.

"For want of kids, I nurture serpents. For now, one being as good as the other, it makes no odds. The annoying thing is that whereas, later on, children become serpents, these ones don't change; they ought to slough off their skin after a certain time and turn into kids. Just look at this nice fat beastie that can't manage any more, how pretty it is with its forked tongue! I love them as if I'd hatched them myself; in any case they do me a favour since they take my milk. To begin with, I was breast-feeding myself, but I soon had enough of that."

And she set up the device she'd had made for her personal use. It was a rubber tube terminating in a little cup, likewise of rubber, the interior of which she would moisten with saliva; she then put this to her breast, and all that was needed was for her to suck the tube a little and some milk would come out.

"I've taken out a patent on my device; if, one day, I have some spare money, I shall exploit it, and it will make me a nice profit. All the nannies will use it without the slightest fear of being woken up during the night by their little moppets; all they need do is fix up my system at bedtime and stuff the tube in the nipper's gob — one sucks while the other sleeps. One of them could sleep on the first floor, the other in the garret; by running the tube along the staircase the set-up will work the same. Better still, out in the street the nurse can leave the little one in its pram; when it howls, she can chuck it the tube and carry on with the outing uninterrupted. And so on. I tell you, it's a cute invention, absolutely first-rate."

"Oh, but it won't get you into the Panthéon!"*

"No, but it might get me into Saint-Lazare. There's always that chance.

Come on now, shall we go to the rehearsal, or rehearse here?"

They opted to rehearse at La Pondeuse's place. And all of an instant, they decked themselves out in tarlatan skirts, pink stockings and pantaloons. Their costumes, cut rather low, brought their delicious curves just into view. With flirtatious off-handedness they tied on ballet shoes and began prancing about. They counted beats by snapping their fingers and pirouetted in time. Their gestures were identical; having the same build, and both dressed alike, they were, it seemed, as one woman split in two. Seeing them, Mauri remembered Mani-Mina, then the way the Duc de la Croix de Berny had appeared in the ballet *The Eyes of Desdemona*. And the fancy took him, in his turn, to dress as a dancer and do the splits.

"Ah, my poor dearie, you're going to look awfully silly in that get-up. But before any of that, do you know how to dance?"

"A little bit."

"Have you not had lessons with Saracco, or with Balbiani? Well then, back to bed with you."

But he insisted. Mademoiselle Jeanne had a stage costume right there in her flat: tights, a tutu, skirts and a corset. The latter in no way resembled the sort our mothers used to wear; so as to allow the graceful bearing of the arms and turning of the torso, it was very low-cut and deeply scooped at the back. The *chemise*, likewise, was unusual; it had no arm-holes, was very low in the front and cut high over the hips and came down to a long point at the back which could then be pulled up between the legs to the front. Mauri wanted to learn the *pas de si-sol*. They told him how to do it.

"With your feet in the fifth position, rise up, *jeté* with the right foot while throwing the left foot backwards, return the left foot behind the right foot, in the fifth, put the right foot behind the left foot, also in the fifth position."

"All those fifth positions? Everything should end up being continuous."

"Where have you danced?"

"At the Bullier."*

The ladies all protested. The Bullier! A disreputable dive where the art of dance was subjected to endless tortures. A frothing sea of heads bathed with lights, heads with but the ghosts of frightful smiles. Here the consciences of the impure take refuge, the rhythm of the waltz offering a place where their misdeeds can be lugged back and forth, thus to descend into their innards and melt away for a night. Then they float back up to the surface again. The women, all devirginised, put on a show of exquisite unconcern beneath the blitheness of their attire; the multiple colours of their grotesque outfits dazzle, and from afar, with their rouge and their flounces all blurred in the reflection from poorly-cleaned mirrors, they bring to mind a confusion of faded flowers. To the Bullier! But everything there is a façade: the dancing, the light, the rhythm of the *entrechats*; the very leaves of the chestnut trees in the garden take on the tints of theatrical scenery, green, a zinc-green faded by the sun. Even the scent the crowd gives off is fake; the sweat of brows, of armpits and crotches, filtered through unwashed skins, smells inhuman. The very atmosphere is adulterated, and this adulteration of the ambient air acts upon people's minds and unhinges them; thus affected, young people lacking in gentility test the strength of their biceps on the stomach of a a mannikin, primed with an internal mechanism that declares its strength as an opponent, but is no more than an empty claim.

"Your education needs seeing to dearie."

Mauri had gone into the living-room to get dressed. A confused murmur was rising from the street. A crowd, gathered just outside La Pondeuse's door, was gazing upwards; all those human phizzes were staring at something. What? A fire?

"It's not as if we're kicking up a great shindy; is it maybe the neighbour woman upstairs, who washes herself starkers?"

It wasn't the neighbour woman upstairs who washes herself starkers. The door to La Pondeuse's room opened and a policeman came in, with brand-new boots on.

"I'm going to run the rotter in! So where is he?"

"Who?"

"A filthy brute who does unmentionable things in front of a window without any curtains. There's kiddies going by; so all right, all the little girls know perfectly well what a naked man looks like, but the law's the law, and it punishes people who put their backsides on view. So hand over that man!"

And he laid hold of Mauri, who was just finishing lacing up his ballet shoes. Impelled by the officer he tumbled four-at-a-time downstairs and was escorted to the station. On the way he skipped like a dragonfly, with his tutu spread out — he had fastened it about his stomach, too high therefore, with the result that he resembled a spinning-top.* His flustered expression, and the blur of his legs, hugely amused the street-urchins and the strollers of the quartier des Écoles.

Arriving at the station:

"What is your name?"

"Mauri de Noirof."

"You're a travelling showman, that's obvious. Where's your permit? You haven't got it. Very well. Where were you born?"

He didn't reply.

"Where do you live?"

He didn't reply.

"Answer, will you, for God's sake! Where were you born?"

"That mishap, superintendent... This will make you laugh. My mother taught me the story by heart."

"Eh?"

"The story of my birth."

So he told it.

One day his mother experienced a notable fit of absent-mindedness.

That day she was seated in a compartment on the Ostend-Basel express.

Absorbed by the magnificence of the panorama unfolding about her, she remembered only as night fell that, as of that morning, she had bestowed on the world one more living being.

She planted a kiss on the rosy cheek of her infant, a boy, as thoroughly ugly as is customary among the new-born. He was gifted with long little legs which he agitated constantly while clinging to the breasts of his nurse, a sturdy country lass who had seen better days and who had the peculiar habit of mislaying everything she laid hands on.

Arriving in Switzerland, the two women found themselves well and truly discomfited: there was no sign of Monsieur de Noirof. The clerk at the Hôtel du Pic Ardent, where they had alighted, suggested that they were perhaps mistaken in coming to his establishment. Madame de Noirof fumbled in her pockets and, as it happened, found there a letter from her husband on headed paper from the Hôtel de la Lune Rousse. This hotel was situated on the far side of town. She made her way there forthwith, leaving nursie and infant at the Pic Ardent. But at the Lune Rousse there was a fresh set-back: her husband had left a week ago. At that moment he was cooling his heels at home in Aubevoye, in Normandy, awaiting his wife's return. Feeling at her wits' end, she got to the station, bought a ticket for the express to Paris and, forty-eight hours later, burst like a bomb into the family home.

"You!" cried Noirof on seeing her again, "I thought you were dead… What's the meaning of this?"

She explained her misadventures with a perfect volubility and charm: she'd got the date wrong and left for Basel a week too late. And she recounted the ups and downs of her visits to Ostend, Flushing and Bruges.

Then, noticing that her husband was eyeing her, all agape, surprised at her vanished pregnancy:

"Ah," she said, "it's true, I forgot to tell you!"

And, resuming the thread of her conversation:

"Picture the scene at Blankenbergue, across the dunes, we were galloping on donkey-back…"

"Where is it?"

"The donkey?"

"No, the child."

"Where is it? But…"

She collected her thoughts… but she had left it back there, with the nurse, she hadn't even thought of bringing them back with her. This was a botheration.

Next day the couple set out for Switzerland.

The proprietor of the Pic Ardent received them with a sigh of relief. So he was finally going to be rid of that bloody brat that had been wailing for two whole days, filling the place with its bawling, and which they'd as near as maybe sent to the foundlings' home. Not seeing any sign of her employer's return, the nurse had set out in search of her; upon discovering that she had left the Lune Rousse, she too had gone homewards, all alone, leaving the new-born child in Basel.

The de Noirof family returned home. To their astonishment, the nurse was not yet at Aubevoye. The unfortunate lass, mistaking the train, had gone the devil alone knows where all round Transylvania and after having surveyed the Carpathians, wound up once more, four days later and with her head in a whirl, back at the Pic Ardent. There was no sign of the clerk, there had been a change of staff; some holiday-makers, together with a baby they left in the hotel while they went for a walk in the town, were occupying the unfortunate girl's room. Without further thought, she took the child, returned to the station, and left for Aubevoye.

Finally she arrived.

"So there you are, Theresa!" (For her name was Theresa.) "What's that you've got there?"

"But it's the little one, Madame."

"Eh? The little one?"

"Damn and blast it!" the husband bellowed. "You got it wrong, the one you picked up isn't yours."

"Right enough," the nurse responded, and told them about the trip to Basel. "It's you that's mistaken, this one really is yours."

The two of them were laid side by side: impossible to tell one from the other.

"He never left my side," Theresa repeated. "You've taken somebody else's child."

"Perhaps it's you, Theresa, that's made the mistake!"

"That's not impossible."

"You can't tell the difference?" the husband asked.

"But no," the wife replied, showing no concern.

She took up her lorgnette:

"They're so alike!"

"Ah, how nice it is to be a father like this."

Then, after an interval:

"You didn't, perhaps, have two?"

 Oh no, as for that she was certain. And all three went at it, hammer and tongs, making no end of a fuss.

It was much worse when the two women each opted for one kiddie or the other.

"It's this one."

"No, it's that one."

"Damn and blast it!" the husband thundered, "there's no knowing which way to turn."

"I've got two ways," said Theresa, unconsciously playing on words, "I'm well up to suckling both."

The neighbours pitched in. Two groups had formed amongst the womenfolk.

"This one has the mother's eyes."

"That one has the father's conk."

They sent telegrams to Basel, to the Pic Ardent, to the police and to the newspapers.

A new difficulty arose. Aubevoye town hall was calling for the new-born infant to be entered into the register of births, deaths and marriages. They sent the village constable round to the Noirofs'.

"Could you wait just a bit," the father said, "the parents of the other one will surely turn up and recognise it."

"That being the case," the constable said, "just register yours, since one of them belongs to you. You're sure of that much, aren't you?"

"I think so, anyhow."

He put the question to his wife:

"You're quite sure of it?"

"Of bloody course!"

But witnesses were needed to authenticate the registration. Where to find them? And, to complicate the situation, the constable chimed in:

"And suppose the others don't recognise their one, what'll you do then?"

Theresa ventured a suggestion:

"We'll draw straws."

They went off to the town hall. All along the way, Noirof continued muttering:

"So much for fatherhood! I'm the father of Lord knows which child!"

Having arrived at the town hall:

"Where was he born?"

"I don't know," said the husband. "My wife is better informed than I am about that."

The mayor repeated the question to the mother.

"In Sweden, in the Telemark."

"What's that? In Sweden?"

"My mistake, it was in England, no, between Ostend and Basel. I think it was between Ostend and Basel."

"Between Ostend and Basel," the official remarked, "you've got Belgium, the grand Duchy, France, Germany and Switzerland. We must be specific. Was he actually just born in France?"

"I no longer remember. At that moment I wasn't looking out of the door. Oh, but it doesn't matter, put down 'Born in a railway-carriage'."

And at that she was delighted; she danced a little jig, her face beaming, and pinched her husband's arm, saying:

"In a railway-carriage! In a railway-carriage! I find that very funny. You too? Go on then, laugh!"

All those present guffawed with laughter, but Noirof, horror-stricken, did not so much as smile. Gravely he announced:

"You're not serious. I shan't be having any more children by you; it's not worth the trouble, seeing as you just lose them."

 "In that case I shall bring the proceedings to a close since no one knows anything here," declared the mayor.

Two days later the other child's parents turned up.

"Our daughter! Our dear daughter!"

A girl! They hadn't thought of that. Both sides were in the clear.

They disendiapered the nippers and redistributed them according to their sexes; then they rediapered them and, to avoid error, labelled them; then they celebrated with a slap-up meal.

During the revelry some prankster swapped the labels.

The result being that, next day, the little male returned to Switzerland, while his parents left for Calvados.

Telegrams sent by both parties remained unanswered, since the parents of the baby girl, back in Zurich, believed Noirof to be in Aubevoye.

After thirty-six days the errors were rectified once and for all.

Mauri de Noirof recited this lengthy speech before the superintendent in a gloomy voice. He summed up:

"When one has come into the world like that, Monsieur, anything can be expected. It affects one's whole life."

"Where do you live?"

"I can't remember the number: on the Rue de Rennes, up on the left, next to a cheesemonger's."

"Are you a travelling showman?"

"Not at all. I do nothing."

"Have you any means of support? Search that man there."

They searched him. He hadn't a brass farthing in his pocket for the simple reason that he had no pockets.

They slung him in the lock-up, in the company of a good few none-too-nice good-for-nothings.

The investigation continued. The police contrived, based on the accused's sketchy clues, to locate his residence. The young bride was there alone, engaged in eating pancakes and laying out a game of patience. As soon as she was informed of the situation, she hastened very slowly to go and fetch her mother and her mother-in-law. They made their way to the station, and there nothing very much was explained. Mauri did not remember anything. They released him none the less, after he had sworn not to re-offend.

"You can't go home like that. Where have you left your things?"

"I don't know."

Hermine gazed at him admiringly:

"Oh but yes! It'd be even better if he went back like this. We aren't bound to dress like everybody else, are we?"

"I wanted to learn an amazing dance-step that featured a large number of fifths. They didn't give me time enough."

"We'll try it at home," said Hermine.

Then, after a little while, she added:

"You weren't very nice to me yesterday. You left me up in the air… It was in my pocket!"

"Eh?"

"The frog."

Since the ladies took their time ascending the stairs in the Rue de Rennes, Mauri raced on ahead, but not having a very clear idea of which floor was which, he rang at doors that slammed shut again noisily, went down, came back up and got lost. He had forgotten the layout of the building and sat down on a divan, convinced that his rhinoceros of a wife would not be long in coming to fetch him. The afternoon went by. Nothing. Tenants came and went, fixing him with mocking stares. He was starving hungry. The concierge found him asleep, and took him home.

Night fell. They went to bed.

"Aren't you going to kiss me?" she asked.

"Wouldn't you prefer me to tickle the soles of your feet?"

"You can try."

He tried. She didn't stir.

"Are you all right, Mauri?"

"I seem to be sliding about on my back. This bed's rickety. And on top of that, it's a box! They really are comfortable, your Breton beds!"

In fact he was rolling down on to his wife. The mattress had a tilt of twenty-two and a half degrees. He couldn't account for this phenomenon. They had to get up to try and find the reason. But it was clear that the mattress was perfectly flat!

"Let's go back to bed."

The see-saw movement began again. Mauri was up in the air and his wife was down below.

"Damn it, I've got it! You're heavier than I am."

So, to counterbalance the load, he put a number of weights on his side, right next to the wall: two twenty-kilo ones, one of five and one that was half a kilo.

She asked:

"Where's your father buried?"

"In Père Lachaise."

"Have you a family grave there?"

"Yes."

"How many places are there left?"

"Three. Why?"

"Because I'd really like to be buried next to you."

"If you were small and slim, we could all squeeze up and make room for you."

Needless to say, she was too fat.

"I'll lose some weight."

She broached another subject:

"You have mistresses, haven't you?"

"A few."

"You'll invite them over ?"

"If you'd like that!"

"Oh yes! I don't want you putting yourself out. You could ask them round now and again to spend an evening with us. We mustn't change your bachelor ways. You don't mind our broaching unusual subjects of conversation on our first night?"

"On the contrary. People who are out of the ordinary don't chatter away like ordinary people. Have you any lovers?"

"I beseech you, Monsieur, to see in me the purest of women."

"Will you have any?"

"The religion of Christ forbids me that. I'm joining my destiny to yours and God alone knows what surprises the future has in store for me. I shall not break my vow, Monsieur. You are, however, a very strange being, and you deserve to be cuckolded all your life long. I have my principles, and they are firmly fixed."

And she tapped her breast a few times which caused her to let out a silent fart under the bed-clothes. A shitty stink simmered away, then diffused through the bedroom, almost asphyxiating them.

"I'm sorry, it's the pancakes. Whenever I eat them, they give me wind."

He asked:

"Have you studied chemistry?"

 "Not in the slightest."

"That surprises me, because I'd have thought you were well up on the subject of hydrochloric acid."

And she said:

"Would you like to be a minister?"

"A minister for what?"

"Anything at all. I'm asking because the portfolio of Public Works is about to fall vacant. The person now in the job is retiring."

"He's retiring from politics?"

"Having made a packet. So I thought, seeing as you're perfectly useless, we could put you up for his position."

In the glow of the night-light, which shed as much illumination as an electric lamp, Mauri cast an eye over his wife. She was curled up in a ball, a sphere some sixty centimetres in diameter. Her eyes had the vague softness of a cow's on the point of calving, and a deep sense of calm froze the lines of her face. From time to time her eyes blinked, and then, next to her temple, a most unattractive tic started twitching, which seemed to have been set in motion by her Nerve of Cunning.

And so married life got under way for the couple. Hermine's dowry allowed Mauri to realise one of his most cherished dreams: he acquired a brougham, four horses, and spent the greater part of his days in having himself driven around Paris quite at random. He would say to Pancrace:

"Take me somewhere or other."

And Pancrace didn't take him anywhere in particular. He whipped up the horses and let them go wherever they fancied. Thus they would on occasion end up wandering into the strangest parts. One evening, in Grand-Montrouge, they came upon a suburban fair, and the sign on one of the booths gave Mauri a start. He decided to return there.

When he got back home, his wife would be there or she wouldn't be there.

Almost every day she absented herself promptly at four in the afternoon, a matter, she said, of going to succour the poor of Saint-Germain-des-Prés. She belonged to a philanthropic society presided over by a fashionable lady, and in that lady's company would offer aid to people in their homes. On returning from these charitable visits, her breath had a strange smell in which there was a hint of aniseed.

When not away from home, she would relax, musing the time away in her living-room with a bottle of eau-de-vie, or cognac, or rum, or chartreuse and a little glass which she constantly refilled. She aimed, by the continued absorption of alcoholic liquids, to combat the obesity which daily, and also weekly, deposited a layer of fat about her physical being.

Their conversations never crossed the borders of the banal. For all that, Hermine was calmer, more settled; she remembered to think before she spoke and her pauses wrapped up her words in a way that masked their emptiness. In reality they spoke in order to say nothing. They were utterly bored.

Madame Israël paid rare visits. Proud though she was at having arranged a marriage for her daughter, she none the less nourished a certain barely concealed scorn for Mauri's mother for having neglected his upbringing. She made no bones about these sentiments, and made frequent allusions to the Noirofs' expensive tastes.

"Why are you still so idle, my dear son-in-law? And why is it your mother leads the life of a duchess? She no longer has the money to justify it. Why does she make such a splash? I still have an income of forty thousand francs, do I put on airs?"

Mauri would reply:

"I'm working on something. Wait a bit, and you'll see. Before long the world will be talking about me."

He sketched out plans for a quadruple dovecote, tore them up and started all over again. Then, one day, he rubbed his hands together briskly: he'd hit upon it.

This concentrated work set his head spinning. He blundered about in his apartment like an empty-headed hornet, knocking into one piece of furniture and rebounding against another. Since the floor was polished he slipped up, on account of the rapidity of his movements and his putting into practice the theory of the straight line: in wanting to pass through everything, he would turn abruptly, at acute angles, or at right angles, according to the external form of the obstacles encountered. His wife watched him, anxious lest he break something or injure himself. She hated anything getting moved from where it belonged, and said with a sigh:

"How can you fidget about like that? It's so much nicer sitting still."

There was nothing they could agree upon. She never went to the theatre, and such was her aversion to music that she stopped up her ears when Mauri, who had a passion for the piano, played some Wagner or Beethoven, his favourite composers. She had no notion of the art of making the best of her feminine charms; she dressed in a slapdash manner, any old how, and this absence of any effort to make herself attractive led her husband to confess his admiration for the exquisitely fastidious way tarts had about them:

"A woman with nice shoes, her black stockings held up smartly, a silk petticoat edged with lace and a slight scent of violet about her — now there's nothing quite like that."

"Since it's from their bodies that they make a living, they have to lead men into temptation."

"There's no difference between a decent woman and a *cocotte*: both were created to make a living out of their bodies. With this difference alone — that a married woman should be more of a *cocotte* than the *cocotte* herself."

Hermine spent her mornings devouring confectionery, reading the serial in the *Petit Journal*, and picking her nose.

"Don't rummage about like that in your nasal organ. It's disgusting. People blow their nose, it's cleaner than nipping out your cakes and eating them."

Whereupon, to irritate him further still, she picked all the more and with the end of her forefinger extracted a thread of snot the length of a piece of spaghetti. Then she rolled it into a ball and swallowed it.

Such minor faults were amply atoned for by the purity of her sentiments. Seeing her, one could divine within a clear conscience, a heart imbued with the sanctity of its duties. She did not lie, she was faithful to her spouse. And this irreproachability in her morals was not to his liking. Since he had mistresses, she was free to take lovers. On this point too, there was a difference of opinions.

That sign on the booth in Grand-Montrouge was running around in his head, and so he went back there. At the junction of three streets lined with acacias he told Pancrace to stop and disappeared into the eddy of sensation-seekers thronging to get a closer look at the extraordinary spectacle. Mauri entered; he saw it and was stupefied. He remained rooted to the spot, an icy sweat chilled his features and it took a superhuman effort to suppress a loud cry. He left and sent for the showman.

"Ah, it's you!" said the fellow, recognising him, "well, you've managed this very nicely!"

"Here's my card; have her come to see me on Sunday afternoon."

And he leapt into his carriage, which departed at a gallop. He was in a hurry to merge into the darkness.

He did not enjoy his dinner at all. Over tea, his mother drew him aside:

"I'm rather short of money. I shall need forty thousand francs to pay an antique-dealer's bill; on top of that I'm a quarter behind with the rent and I'm inviting the Bishop of Djurdjura to lunch soon."

He wrote a cheque for a hundred thousand francs.

"If that's not enough…"

"I'll try to make do. Anyhow, if I'm short of anything… Are you happy in your new home?"

"I don't know. I still haven't had time to think about that."

Hermine was sulking.

"So what's bothering you, dear lady?"

"I made a hash of it. Just now, going collecting for charity, I went into a smart colour-merchant's and he laughed in my face."

"Why?"

"Come on now, you know perfectly well. The first time you came to us on the Boulevard Saint-Germain, you remarked that my portrait lacked a certain dewiness. I thought about that for days, and I said to myself: next time you pass a shop that sells artists' materials, buy some dewiness and steep your portrait in it. But, you know what, they don't sell tubes of dewiness! I swear to you I was vexed, ever so vexed."

The household was run extravagantly. Hermine was doling out any amount of money to her poor, while the staff, who were numerous, stuffed themselves and boozed mightily when their employers' backs were turned. For his part, Mauri, in pursuing his secret designs, had purchased in Bourg-la-Reine a ten-hectare plot, twenty metres wide, and as a consequence very long. He took on forty teams of labourers and the work would take exactly a month.

"What work?"

"Ah, there you go!"

He said no more about it. His wife noticed that, at certain times of the day, he would wander about pensively, his head hunched between his shoulders, his eyes fixed on the ground. His gaze seemed to pierce the floors and ceilings of all the floors beneath and penetrate deep into the ground. Sometimes he would transport the physicality of his own being about the streets of the left bank, his brougham following at a respectful distance. It was thus that Mauri went on his way, brewing up ideas and moving his lips, his head bent like that of a man condemned to take a census of all the gobbets of spittle that spangle the pavements of Paris.

Sunday came. He received a laconic note:

"I be in you plays at tree-clock. M.M." He sent his staff away, hoping thus to find himself at home alone, since his wife usually made herself scarce after lunch to go visiting the sick. This Sunday though, exceptionally, she did not go out. To complete the imbroglio, Madame Israël turned up at a quarter past two, or two-seventeen, as did his mother, Madame de Noirof. The ladies had decided to make pancakes and spend the day with the family. Besides, it was pelting with rain, weather unfit even for chucking the dog out.

"I promise," Mauri said again, "that you'll all be doing me a favour leaving me on my own here today. I'm expecting some men from the ministry and have to show them the plans for my big machine. It's annoying to have womenfolk around when one wants to discuss serious matters."

"But we won't show ourselves, you can have your meeting in the living-room. You can carry on as if we weren't here."

The doorbell rang. Mauri leapt up as if he'd trodden on sword-points. He went to open up, taking care to close all the doors behind him. In the half-open doorway he could make out the smudged features of a coalman carrying a weighing-machine on his shoulders.

"Madame de Noirof. Thish the addresh?"

"Yesh, that's right." Mauri called Hermine, who had ordered the weighing-machine to go in her bedroom.

"I shall weigh myself every morning, my dear; I shall make a note of my weight before and after my motion. I shall likewise record the fluctuations of my plumpness. I have bought a notebook-ledger-day-book in which I shall keep an account of my fatness. Sorry, but we all need our hobbies!"

Ten minutes later there was another ring on the doorbell. It was her. He ushered her in with the utmost discretion, and with a finger to his lips said:

"Careful! Not a sound. There are people here. I don't want them to know…"

And, out loud: "Ah, do come in, gentlemen!"

She didn't understand a word. "I'm not gentlemen."

"Then be quiet!" And he shut the living-room door.

A great silence ensued.

"What can they be talking about?" Hermine repeated. "Let's listen at the door!"

And they queued up to find out what the great secret was. They could hear arguing in the living-room and someone was weeping, the sound of a woman's sobs.

"But my darling, you won't abandon it, promise me? To think of it, what a calamity! You know full well it's yours. And if it comes to term, you will look after it? I'd like you to promise that before I die. My God, my God, what a calamity!"

A dry cough punctuated these lamentations.

"I'll take care of it, I promise. I didn't know you were pregnant. You ought to have got rid of it."

"No, for soon I must die. At least I shall know the pleasures of maternity, I shall see our child. I'm to give birth in a week or so. And when it's a fortnight old then I shall die. Oh God, what a calamity!"

The three women had their ears glued to the door. A child! That beast of a man had gone and given some woman a child! And here he was, welcoming her under their roof! They heard kisses, along with the clink of coins. He was giving her money! For her confinement, no doubt. And he'd take care of the child!

"We'll see about that," said Hermine. "Let's go in, I want to see."

They went in.

A human monstrosity was what they saw. It was Mani-Mina. An advanced state of pregnancy filled out her right side; but the left side, wasted away by a galloping consumption, resembled a skeleton. Mauri stammered out the beginning of a confession.

"There are accidents that happen unexpectedly... Every man has his weak points... A moment of forgetfulness comes upon one so suddenly..."

"What a revolting thing!" Hermine cried. "Fancy getting involved with such a horror!"

"Come on now," Mani and Mina protested. "You really ought to take a look at yourself. And what's it to you anyhow?"

"But this man is my husband."

"And then what? I'm still pregnant, aren't I?"

Madame de Noirof intervened: the poor unfortunate was right, it was unfair to blame her, and the three women ended up feeling pity for her. The rain was drumming against the windows; from a sooty sky there filtered a diffuse light which barely illuminated the shapeless furniture in the living-room and the human bipeds shuffling about. Mina was spitting blood, her sister felt pains in her lower abdomen; they could no longer stand up, climbing the stairs had worn them out. Collapsing on the sofa, they wailed convulsively, their eight limbs intertwining like the tentacles of an octopus.

"Poor little sister," said Mina, "it's me that's making you die. What breaks my heart is that I can't kiss you and ask your forgiveness."

Their heads could not, in fact, approach each other since the spine was inflexible.

"Still," Mina went on, "we've got another three weeks yet. We'll pray every day that God may forgive our error."

She was overcome by a bout of coughing.

"I'd so much like to lie down."

And she lost consciousness, with a small reddish thread trickling from the corner of her mouth.

"Get them to the hospital!"

"Never! We'll look after them here."

It was decided they should remain at the Rue de Rennes until the delivery.

There followed an outburst of loving kindness, an exaggerated eagerness to help, bustling comings and goings and a display of extravagant pity. The doctor, the midwife, the pharmacist were all conscripted; they set tisanes a-steeping, they applied leeches, they administered clysters. They wanted to save the baby.

"What'll become of the poor little thing?" Mani asked.

"I'll bring it up," Hermine answered. "Don't worry about that. Die in peace."

They spoke about death as if talking about something of no great importance. They discussed the decomposition of bodies, the worms that gnawed them and the stinking gruel that besmeared the wood of coffins when the corpses grew over-ripe. It was particularly at mealtimes that they chose to consider such matters.

Meanwhile, Mauri's excitability was becoming more pronounced. Every morning, after kissing Mani, he set off for Bourg-La-Reine. Work had begun there and a tunnel was being dug in the ten-hectare plot. Things were progressing at a cracking pace. As there were three times the number of workers needed at any one time, teams relieved each other every half-hour. They excavated soil, put in pit-props, they laid bricks, laid rails, slaved away and didn't take time off to eat. Hermine's dowry was eaten up in a week. So as not to halt progress Madame Israël had to fork out three hundred thousand francs, then two hundred thousand francs, then a hundred thousand francs. She hardly had time to draw breath: her son-in-law was bleeding her bank account dry.

"You'll be the ruin of me."

"Leave off! In a month you'll be raking in millions."

He had obtained authorisation from the Ministry to conduct the celebrated experiments he talked about only evasively at home. The minister, along with an *ad hoc* committee, would be present. There wouldn't be a soul left in Paris that day. Everybody would be going to Bourg-La-Reine.

"I'd rather not tell you anything. You'll read about it in the papers."

One day he ran into Jardisse. The man's nose was much longer — it was getting to be a real proboscis.

"You have a charming wife."

"You know her, then?"

Jardisse blushed.

"No, but I've heard tell."

"Oh, charming! Not quite absolutely..."

"She's too fat, in fact."

"You've seen her!"

"Someone told me."

"Come and have dinner one evening, tomorrow, for example; you can make her acquaintance."

"I'd be delighted. By the way, I came out without any money; could you just lend me a couple of hundred?"

And while Mauri was fumbling in his pockets, Jardisse said: "It's wonderful to be able to help people. When I was rich it was my great failing that I always turned away anyone asking for money. I see now that charity is a fine and noble thing, and I regret, damn it, not having practised it in days gone by."

He shook Mauri's hand lingeringly, while tickling his palm with a finger-tip.

"What do you mean by that strange hand-shake?"

"Would you let me give you a kiss?" Jardisse replied.

And he stared Mauri in the eyes most impudently.

"Give me a kiss?"

"To thank you for the service you've just rendered me."

"I'd prefer it if you paid me back my money one day."

"Oh, you can count on me, good fellow, as far as that's concerned."

 Hermine pulled a face when she heard Jardisse was coming to dine the next day.

"The idea of inviting that man! He disgusts me. He has a nasty look about him. They say he's a sodomite. If he comes here, people will take the two of you for a pair of nancy-boys. And anyhow, he's a thief, he's up to his eyeballs in debt and he borrows left, right and centre…"

"You know him, then?"

"No, but I'm on visiting terms with plenty of ecclesiastics; Jardisse, who was brought up in the bosom of the Catholic Church, has lots of connections in the world of priests and has exploited every one of them. There are those who tell me these things. You know him, in any case — he robbed your mother. What an idea, inviting him!"

The idea was indeed stupid; they had trouble enough with their patients and with the tunnel business, without condemning themselves to be bothered at table by people they hated. Jardisse turned out to be a boor; he served himself first, didn't pass the plate to anybody, spoke with his mouth full, sending scraps of chewed this-and-that into neighbouring plates and glasses, sitting with his elbows on the table while noisily picking out the food debris lodged between his teeth. His conversation was brusque and disagreeable; it was an idler's way of speaking, or a failure's, an envious creature condemned to parasitism by his indolence. He was put out that not everybody was like him. He thought all men were just stupid *cunts*, above all those who, by dint of working, had made a livelihood for themselves, or who had lent him money. Hermine sent him packing.

A few days later, the *Journal Officiel* published the following brief para:

An experiment — in the presence of His Majesty the King, the entire cabinet, and delegations from both Chambers along with the École Polytechnique — will take place tomorrow at Bourg-La-Reine, at eleven in the morning. An engineer, M. Mauri de Noirof, claims to have invented a means of railway transport capable of travelling a thousand

*times more rapidly than the best of our express trains. The King will
arrive at eleven a.m. precisely.*

Getting on for two million spectators were lined up that day between Bourg-La-Reine and Antony-et-Berny. The valley of the Bièvre* vanished beneath the mass of men and women who had come along in order to see something. They saw nothing. No visible evidence betrayed the slightest preparation for the experiment. Only a single chimney, two hundred metres high, stood majestically perpendicular beside the L'Hay highway, trailing plumes of black, very black smoke. And that's all there was, a chimney with plumes of black, very black smoke. No sign at all of a railway. They understood not a thing, but enjoyed themselves immensely. The visitors from Paris were happy enough, they'd been sold a pup. They were rejoicing, larking about, when army bugles suddenly announced the arrival of the Head of State and the official party. The King and his retinue made their way underground. Then they reappeared. Then they disappeared. Everybody went back to Paris. They'd seen nothing.

The Minister for Public Works told Mauri: "I have set aside from my secret funds almost a million francs to assist you in bringing this endeavour to a most successful conclusion. I shall see that a special budget of fifty million gets voted through by the Chamber in order that it may be developed on the grand scale, as with the Paris-Lyon, for example. It only remains to say that the profits will be split equally between us."

A contract was then agreed on between de Noirof and the government, under the terms of which the former retained the exclusive monopoly on the exploitation of his discovery.

 Meanwhile, Mani's time was approaching. Abdominal pains gnawed at her insides and she writhed in her labour, even as Mina, scarcely breathing, faded slowly away. The jolts and kicks her little one gave on the brink of coming into the world were wearing her out and hastening her end. Her body, wasted by the lupus, was haemorrhaging badly; the doctor sought to stem the bleeding, for form's sake, using an iodoform ointment that stank abominably.

Mauri asked the doctor: "When'll it be?"

"The child will be here in two hours."

"And her?"

"She'll go perhaps even before then."

They hurried to fetch a priest. Mina received the last rites, but Mani refused them. She called for Hermine:

"What'll become of the poor little thing?"

"Well… we'll bring it up."

"Will you be suckling it?"

"Can't be done, I'm still a heifer."

But Mauri, fumbling in the pocket of his frock-coat, came upon the little piece of brick he'd picked up so long ago on the Boulevard de Montrouge, and this piece of brick reminded him of La Pondeuse. La Pondeuse reminded him of suckling the grass snakes, suckling the grass snakes reminded him of the celebrated doctor who induced milk in the breasts of even women who were sterile. In two shakes he was with La Pondeuse who led him right away to the doctor in question, Messé-Malou. Messé-Malou lived in Bel-Air in a house with no windows, with a single massive oak door studded with huge, square, pointed nails.

"Can people see properly in there?"

"The house has three storeys and there's more light on the ground floor than in the street outside. There's light even in the cellar. And yet there's not a single window. Messé-Malou didn't want any — it's him who had the house built — so's to pay the least possible taxes. He does have a point, you know."

They went in.

"Be quick about it." Messé-Malou said. "What is it that you want from me?"

"There's a woman who's about to die in childbirth, and the child will have to be fed by a woman who has no milk."

"Where is she, this woman who has no milk?"

True enough, they had forgotten to bring Hermine with them.

"Never mind about that. Are you the husband?"

"I am that in fact," Mauri replied.

"Will you stand in for your wife? Then you won't have to come back and bother me again. The operation can be done in no time at all."

He examined Mauri's thumb, all the while jabbering away in Latin and scientific jargon: "… precordial region of the gringatory molossos… stirpfiric golgomerus… amphibolic carbonate… acrobatic porphyry… clitoria ternata… vegetalious bismuth…"

"I'm going to inject you in your thumb left and big right toe… I mean in your left thumb and right big toe, with a culture of lactiferous vibrios;* after ten minutes you'll have more milk than a cow."

He called an assistant.

"Bring me the culture at the decillionth dilution, temperature of 44 degrees meridional longitude, and quick about it."

A simple injection was given in thumb and toe.

"Stroll about a bit in the garden, and don't leave until I've assured myself of the success of the operation."

And it was an extraordinary garden Dr. Messé-Malou had. Everything in it was abnormal. There were transparent plants, with black leaves, then some rose-trees that had pears for fruit and further on, some leafless shrubs with aerial roots, a plum tree fruiting with paper spirals and green roses flowering on strawberry plants.

"So, you find this entrancing, do you?" the scientist enquired. "Ah, but you haven't seen anything yet. Come with me — I'll show you my hothouses."

And he led the way. Mauri noticed that his hair was blue, and his head very small; no doubt it had all been used up by thinking. The doctor walked quickly, even though he was ninety-seven.

"Yes, Monsieur, in three years I'll be a hundred. And then I'll start living over again — I'm not going to die. I've solved the problem of the indestructibility of matter. There is no God. Man is the Creator. See for yourself!"

The first hothouse gave the impression of an exhibition of artificial vegetables; there were strange trees that produced, by way of fruits, bunches of iron, copper or tempered steel, others wool, ears of wheat or smoking tobacco.

"In a fortnight this briar rose will yield chewing tobacco. And here are the gold-and the silver-trees."

These were palm trees which secreted drops of gold or silver.

"They bring in on average two thousand francs a day; were I to increase cultivation a hundredfold, I'd see more than seventy million in profit per annum — but I'm careful not to do that as it would lead to a drop in the price of gold. Be so good as to note that not many would be as scrupulous as myself. Ah! Science borders upon the Infinite. I slaved away, Monsieur, for ten and a half, indeed nearly eleven years, before discovering the secret of how minerals are formed. Here is a block of marble which grows bigger and bigger from one day to the next. Not many people know that stones can be cultivated in the same way as simple cereal crops; marble, in common with other minerals, is made up of animalcula which reproduce like crab-lice, with each generation overlaying the previous one as it dies and then solidifies. Once this principle has been established, all that remains is to identify the animalcule. It's a long job — no doubt about that — but if one perseveres, one's time won't be wasted. I have managed it, even if I wasn't the first. And now I'm going to show you something quite brilliant: a man-tree."

And they went into the second hothouse, a pentagonal building encircled all the way round by copper points heavily charged with electricity.

"I've cut off the current, otherwise we'd have been struck down. Those copper points are intended to kill anyone attempting to sneak in here and rob me of my children."

A fantastic vision left Mauri awestruck.

In the middle of the hothouse stood a tree on the branches of which there sprouted human bodies, some in the early stages of formation and others almost fully formed. The trunk of this tree was like any other tree-trunk, but its leaves, which were square, had the same thickness and polish as a section of leather strap, with microscopic valves whose rapid movements indicated the respiration of the beings dangling there, in the air, like hanged men. The branches were sturdy, and each bore only one human fruit. These were attached at the head, by means of a stem that broke off when the body was fully grown. But the doctor could always intervene, if he so chose, to prevent the stem from breaking and so leave the individual still hanging from its branch, even for quite some time. In this way there was a four-month foetus, a two-year-old child, another of six, a third one of ten years. A remarkably attractive young girl of sixteen was conversing with a bearded, pipe-smoking man, well past his thirtieth year. The tree had thirteen branches, and each branch produced a different nationality: French, English, Greek, Russian, Scandinavian, Italian, Hungarian, Spanish, Chinese, Japanese, all were represented there. The collection was completed by a blind man, a deaf mute and a decapitated man.

"How the devil do you get people to grow on a tree?"

"That's both difficult and tricky to explain. Had you made a thorough

study of botany, or even a superficial one, you'd know that each of a plant's roots corresponds to a branch of the same plant. The root nourishes the branch. If you immerse a root in a bath of shit, for example, and keep it there, the fruits of the branch fed by that root will reek of turds. And so on. Well now, substitute for that shit a thick layer of sexual organs, and the fruit obtained from that source of nourishment will obviously be of the same kind as the sexual organs. I mean, of course, sexual organs endowed with fecundatory properties. Otherwise, nothing doing! You understand what I'm driving at? Well, I succeeded in obtaining — and at considerable cost, good God! — a sufficient quantity of organs, buried them in the ground and then pushed the roots of a cypress in amongst them: you see the result! Each of these individuals speaks a different language, but they all understand French, with the exception of the deaf mute and the decapitated one."

"How do you feed them?"

"By pissing at the foot of the tree."

"Oh, damn and blast it!" Mauri exclaimed. "My chest is all soaked with some sort of liquid!"

It was his breasts, which, overflowing, had burst open and were spurting milk.

"There you are now," said Messé-Malou, "you're in a fit state to suckle. Goodbye, and I trust I'll see you again. If one day you start feeling a little gaga, come back and see me. I can give you a venous injection of my regenerative liquor, which renews the nerves and renders them impermeable to wear and corruption. Quick, off you go now."

Then he called him back:

"Be sure to put a little caramel on your nipples, so the little one sucks right away."

"It's either one thing or the other," said La Pondeuse when they had left, "either we've been dreaming and all the enchantments we've just seen will vanish when we awake, or else we're not dreaming at all, and so all we need do is go along with the flow. What's the point of struggling against life, when life's going to win anyway! When it comes to the secret of immortality, or the mystery of how man was created, universal fame can be acquired without recourse to God any more. That doctor is either more powerful than the Lord, or he's a charlatan. As for me, I feel twisted up inside and it ends up making me want to spit in the face of everyone I meet."

"And me, I'm bursting with energy. If I had a stone in my hands, I'd strangle it. What a strange life we're leading!"

"Just a moment! I've got a feeling I saw your wife going into that house over there!"

"But you don't know what she looks like!"

"Didn't I see her in Saint-Germain-des-Prés on your wedding day? But I must be mistaken, what sort of hanky-panky would she be getting up to round here?"

"A long time ago I was obsessed by the idea that a man might impregnate a tree; I'd even willingly have married a plant, but my sainted old bag of a mother, who I love to distraction, persuaded me not to. Messé-Malou is no more powerful than me. It wasn't him who thought up my tunnel!"

Then he opened his little notebook and re-read the word *guillotine*, written one evening while he was whispering sweet nothings to Mademoiselle Israël.

"Another invention that will make a name for me! Godalbloodymighty, what a bloody fine fellow I am!"

Upon getting back home he found a letter from the Head of State, summoning him to the Élysée with the utmost urgency. He arrived with his head in a whirl, with no idea of why he'd been asked to come along. The cabinet had resigned following a vote of no confidence in the Chamber, and they had sent for Noirof to offer him the portfolio of Justice. He accepted.

"But, your kindest and most generous Majesty," he demurred, "to become a minister, one must first be a deputy…"

"And you have been, for a week Monsieur!"

Yes, a deputy for a week. And what's more, deputy for Montrouge! He no longer remembered; his nerves were calming down again, his brain turning to soup. They had to remind him that, after the Bourg-la-Reine experiment, he had been named as the candidate to replace one of the deputies in Montrouge, and had been elected unanimously.

"Don't you remember," Hermine said to him, "the night you tickled the soles of my feet? We talked about the possibility of your name being put forward as head of some ministry or other. It's the Bishop of Djurdjura who's been in charge of all that. You can see how well he's done."

She was looking out of the window as she reminded him of these things, and Mauri thought he saw her trying to exchange significant glances with a passer-by who looked extraordinarily like an individual she cordially detested.

"And Mani-Mina?"

"It'll be another nine months before she gives birth. It seems she must carry the baby twice as long as other women. She's double, so it's only right her gestation period should be double."

"What about my milk, then?"

Then he remembered La Pondeuse's suckling-system. He settled into his post at the Ministry, taking along this device, and office heads and workers came to him in their turn to suckle. It was scandalous. Mauri frequently got into a muddle, and would mistake his device for his speaking tube; he would blow into it and bellow "Allo, allo!" then naturally receiving no response he'd storm about in his office, railing at his staff.

One day he received a visit from the face-slapping artist. The poor fellow had come asking for any old job that would allow him to leave his cheeks in peace for the rest of his days.

"They'll fall off if I go on cuffing them about. Seeing as how I made you laugh when you were only an ordinary tax-payer like myself, surely you could find me something, anything at all, executioner's assistant, for example."

"Executioner's assistant! Executioner's assistant! What an idea!"

And he took out his little notebook.

"See that word there?"

The man couldn't read.

"It's the word *guillotine*, my good fellow. God almighty, but you've put your finger right on it!"

He had a draft bill drawn up concerning the repeal of the penalty ordinarily incurred for adultery, wherein he substituted a punishment unique in the annals of mankind. He then presented the case for his bill to the Chamber in a speech in which the abbreviation of words provoked eddies of barracking, from left, right and centre. He began thus: "Messieus, the gov of the Rep must not negl any opp to amel the mor sit of the peep." The keeper of the record was quite nonplussed and, amongst those assembled, a calm set in that resembled a congealing silence. "Yes, Mess," he continued. "God said one day: 'Thou shalt be puni in the place where thou hast sinned.' Well now, here b'low, the resp to crim is not alw in acc with the div guid." An uproar in F major greeted this maiden speech, but the speaker's hand-bell succeeded in silencing the assembly. Mauri was told to start again, but this time with a pronunciation that could be understood: "I have noticed that all our speeches have a length that is kilometric many times over. Why not shorten them by cutting words in half?" Then he continued, jabbering away, correcting his sentences when he slipped in repetitions. "My apologies, the word 'unfaithful' occurred twice in the part of the sentence I just spoke, let me correct that." And he replaced the repeated word with a synonym. His bill was passed unanimously in its entirety. The main paragraph was worded as follows: "Whosoever shall be convicted of adultery will be obliged to submit to the partial amputation of the organ with which the crime has been committed. The amputation shall not exceed one centimetre. In the event of recidivism, the amputation will be of two centimetres. The model of the instrument of punishment presented before the government is the one that has been adopted."

This instrument had the shape of a miniature guillotine, without of course the tipping-board. The uprights measured two metres, fifty-three and a half centimetres in height; the bevel-edged blade was as sharp as a razor manufactured to shave the downy hairs on the thighs of a pretty young woman, a brunette for preference, and weighed fifty kilogrammes; a catch released it, exactly like the steely justiciary of the scaffold. The lunette was five centimetres in diameter; it slid perpendicularly between two grooves, in such a way that it could always be positioned to match the height of the offender's body.

The cat's-tail eater was appointed executor of the new law. This provoked in him a fit of side-splitting mirth inexpressible in any other language. He spent whole days in La Roquette, consulting earnestly with Deibler,* who instructed him in the working of the new machine. They were often to be seen at daybreak, walking together, deep in discussion and gesticulating, in black frock-coats and gloves, with mourning-bands on their hats. The way they spoke was ghoulish, and the vague odorous sanguinolence of future executions set their tongues salivating and chop-licking like a pair of epicures.

"I am as nothing compared to you," the slap-artist would say.

"Extremes meet," Deibler would respond.

They would laugh, and their laughter had the rippling melody of skeleton bones rattling together.

Mauri de Noirof took his ministerial role seriously. He signed decrees, appointments and dismissals, granted audiences and listened to petitions in a stiff, very stiff, excessively stiff attitude, making no decisions, sending his staff off at a gallop in the hurry to be alone in his office, standing in front of a mirror, pulling faces at himself in full dress, with a little pair of scales in each hand. It was only his milk that was a bit of a bother. To spare his inferiors the unpleasant duty of sucking on his breasts, he employed a little black boy who performed the task whenever the need made itself felt, and whose skin turned café-au-lait as a result. Would Mani-Mina ever piss out her nipper?

From time to time he would turn up at the Rue de Rennes. One evening he surprised his wife in a strange costume: she'd had a minister's wife's coat made and was trying to dance a jig, with a tutu strapped on over the coat — Mauri's tutu. He regarded her with a malign delight; Hermine was having all the trouble in the world just moving, she would rise up, fall back rhinocerously, with the gait of an itinerant barrel, or rather a hippo in labour, or even more, a Guernsey cow the worse for drink.

"I thought you more sober-minded, Madame."

"I'm doing a bit of gymnastics, Minister. And besides, I feel all wound up — your mother came and had a go at me, accusing me of playing the flirt in order to make you fall in love with me; she was here with Madame Israël and they were tearing each other's hair out. You ought to put your foot down; your mother is jealous, and she hates mine, who's made so many sacrifices and almost been reduced to beggary. Fortunately my uncle has just died, and we'll be inheriting six hundred thousand francs. Tra-la-la!"

"And what of your paupers? Are you still looking after them? I do trust that the nobility of your soul, drowned in the torrent of honours with which I am inundated, has lost nothing of its immensity?"

"I visit my paupers as always, that's all I do; then I dress Mani-Mina's sores; then I weigh myself and take my little drop of spirits (I've ordered in seventeen casks so as not to be caught short) because I still feel the odd pain in the teeth of my little gobby-wob. And you, you great idiot, what are you doing, harnessed to the chariot of the State?"

"I'm pulling it. We all pull as best we can. Each one pulls for himself. I've got my hands on the secret budget, so there's always that to fall back on."

"I'm pregnant, Monsieur le Ministre."

"Oh, and by whom?"

"By you, of course!"

He racked his poor noddle, but could not recall any occasion that might account for this pregnancy.

"Am I ill perhaps?"

He scanned various specialised works, made a deeper study of memory disorders and therein read things that filled him with despair: "Every impression leaves a certain indelible mark, that is to say that the molecules, once arranged otherwise and made to vibrate differently, will no longer revert to their exact original state." Should the Mind then be the same forever? His mind, at least. Was there a boiling ferment in his brain every time its molecules were disarranged by the arrival of a new idea? "And yet," he told himself, "I have as many brain cells as anyone else!" According to Meynert* he possessed a minimum of six hundred million, one for each memory. "But if that's so, what if I disturbed them!" As it turned out, there were discharges. "Discharges constantly flash through the nervous system." He was vibrating inside his head! What a man! He was the opposite of so many others!

 The tunnel business was assuming an extraordinary importance. The trial with the Paris-Lyon route had been successful. A train had eaten up the distance in seventeen seconds, smoothly and without any mishap. This invention, which enabled the government, in the event of war, to transport the entire French army to the German border in fifteen minutes, was kept a close secret — alas revealed by a newspaper's indiscretion. It had struck Mauri de Noirof one day how quickly messages could be transmitted by means of pneumatic tubes; he said to himself: "What would happen if a bigger tube was built and the message was replaced by a train?" It was a complete revolution for means of transport on land. A train could travel thirty kilometres in a second, with no need for either fuel or a locomotive, just a single compartment, two or three hundred metres long, would suffice. Passengers climbed aboard, and bang! By the time they'd taken their seats and drawn six and a half normal breaths, they were at their destination. Instead of the thirty-four francs, seventy centimes they normally paid for the privilege of being dragged along for seventeen hours in the third-class from Paris to Lyon, they'd only have to fork out thirty-five *sous*. The journey there and back took a minute. Fifty or sixty thousand residents of Lyon — civil servants for the most part — who were allowed a ninety-minute lunch-break, lost no time in spending it in Paris. They then came back and returned to their jobs. After a month the population of Lyon was reduced to eighteen thousand; the rest had moved to Paris. Paris was bursting with life.

This upheaval coincided with a very serious communication delivered to the Academy of Medicine by Messé-Malou. All the sovereigns of Europe were present, with the exception of those well known for being enemies of France. The subject was The Rejuvenation of Mankind. The celebrated doctor brought before the assembly several individuals more than a hundred years old who enjoyed the vigour, good health, litheness and youthful bloom of twenty-year-olds. This return to their youth had been achieved by infusing the bloodstream with vitalin, a concentrated solution obtained by crushing the head of a living child; from this medium certain cultures of bacilli could be extracted, shaped like semi-colons, which then raced through the subject's body and in so doing renewed the nerves, metallising them, as it were, removing any possibility of wear and tear and protecting against illness. Vitalin caused a severed leg, a lost tooth or eye, or a nose destroyed by the pox, to grow again; any attempts at suicide or murder using ordinary fire-arms would prove impossible. Consequently, any battle initiated against France by her enemies could never work out to the latters' advantage. Those rulers present insisted that experiments should be carried out forthwith. A detachment of the 20th Chasseurs tried in vain to shoot one of the rejuvenated veterans; the bullets tore through his flesh, which then healed immediately. Following this object lesson, general disarmament was agreed upon throughout Europe.

The disturbance brought about by these two events sent shock-waves round the world.

Humanity turned to jelly.

When she arrived she would first of all wish the ailing concierge a good day, then go up to the mezzanine floor and either ring or not ring the bell; she would ring if, having fumbled in the tassel of the bell-pull, she could not find the key; if the key was there, she didn't ring. Three-quarters of the time she didn't ring. The dear fellow was loafing about somewhere in the neighbourhood. Once he had eaten, very well, for twenty-three or twenty-four *sous* at a questionable restaurant on the Boulevard Saint-Michel, he'd hurry off to play a game of poker at the François Premier, with drinks at twelve or fifteen *sous* a glass. He regularly lost fifteen to twenty louis in the course of an afternoon; he would return, at four, to pocket the readies she brought him.

The lodging looked out on to the Rue d'Assas facing the maternity hospital. The shrieks of the unfortunates could be clearly heard, as science induced them to piss out the greybeards' seed they carried inside them. They were the yowls of stray cats or rabid dogs, the howls of antediluvian brutes, which not even a genius could have transcribed into musical notation. From time to time, in the intervals between these noises, the first wails of new-born infants could be heard; the heads of junior doctors would appear at the windows, between a couple of tea-urns. The whiff of pharmaceutical smells, borne by the easterly wind, infested the neighbourhood.

She would tidy up the grubby rooms a little, where an utter disorder always reigned. Then she would wait, sprawled on a sofa, slowly undressing since they always went to bed, a matter of spending *a few pleasant moments* together. For all that, it wasn't the lure of lechery that led her into sin, she didn't experience the faintest pleasure in her surrenders, which were unfuelled by any passion; they indulged the lusts of their flesh as they might have carried out any other tiresome duty. He would arrive and kiss her, each time repeating the same sentence: "You are a saintly woman." He'd tell of his bad luck at cards: he always lost.

"Get out of the habit then!" she would repeat. He would promise, gamble again that evening or the next day, trying again to be rid of it. However, he was obeying a compulsion he was powerless to fight off. She would hand over three or four hundred-franc notes which, of course, he would take. He'd say:

"I'm up to my neck in debt; this three hundred francs couldn't come at a better time. First up, I won't pay my tailor; then I won't pay the two months' hire for my harmonium. I've borrowed three louis from so-and-so and won't pay that back."

No, he wouldn't be paying a thing, he'd be leaving his debts in peace. On the other hand, he still retained a passion for bric-a-brac, and few indeed were the days when he did not bring back some object to add to his collection. His apartment was cluttered with a jumble of paintings, crucifixes, plaster saints, plates, rickety pieces of furniture, chairs of every style, carpets, muskets and old books. The harmonium had pride of place and since he played only religious music, chanting in Latin and with a little skullcap on his head, she would imagine herself in a chapel, and sometimes, in her nakedness, kneel down and pray out loud.*

After dressing, she'd go downstairs with her hair uncovered, to the greengrocer's, the baker's, the butcher's, the wine-merchant's, to fetch him his dinner. For she had to go home; it was rare for her to spend the evening there. And she would leave as casually as when she had arrived.

114

"These daily absences — what does your husband make of it?"

"I let him believe I'm visiting the poor. But I nearly gave myself away the other day. I spoke ill of you, I told him you were a nobody. 'You know him then?' he said. 'No,' I said, 'but so I'm told.' 'He's an odd sort,' he said. 'Oh, I can't stand him,' I said. 'He's coming to dinner tomorrow.' 'Oh really,' I said, 'you're inviting a pervert, a proper mess you've made there!' I made a show of being annoyed, but deep down I was so happy. Oh, but he's a long way from imagining we know each other."

"You are a saintly woman."

But one day she realised she was pregnant, and that was a nuisance.

"We never sleep together. How am I going to get him to swallow this?"

"That's perfectly simple: he's an amnesiac, just convince him the child is his."

And, in fact, Mauri did believe that he was the father.

"Never," she said, "have I known a household like ours. Since he became Minister, it's been one thing after another. Not to mention that freak from the Hippodrome, who whinges from morning to night, and who still hasn't dropped it. I'm all at sea. You know, life shouldn't be as difficult as this. It'll drive us mad and we'll end up dying in a lunatic asylum."

Summer came. For a long time he'd been badgering her to spend some time at the seaside.

"But what if my husband comes too?"

"Suggest it to him; you know exactly how he'll reply."

Mauri said to Hermine:

"The sea air is bound to be good for you, so go. It's better you aren't here when Mani-Mina gives birth. But you must be back when the Bishop of Djurdjura honours us with his visit, as arranged for August. It's now the middle of May. Pick a resort where there are lots of trees, flowers and greenery; perhaps I'll come along and relax for a day or two, but later on, not now. Just now I'm drawing up my budget. And, you know, a budget…"

But he wasn't drawing up a budget: he was in love. Their trysts took place on the Rue Tronson du Coudray, in a ground-floor apartment immortalised by a famous murder case.*

Mauri de Noirof had succeeded in acquiring some of the exhibits produced in the course of the trial: the famous trunk, in which the perfumes and fine linen had been packed; the cord she wore around her waist; the sack, used for the dust-sheet of the easy chair in whose arms she settled her divine figure; the pulley, set in motion by tying a gingerbread man to it as a counterweight. To make the scene of the crime more authentic Mauri had obtained some pig's blood and spattered it over the walls and the floor. Skulls and bones adorned the ceilings in the different rooms, and on a gloomy day, dark as the Conscience of Mankind, the apartment would resemble a tomb.

They experienced the height of intoxication on visiting the place every Friday and on the thirteenth of each month. Mauri arrived first; he drew the shutters and lit the green-glass lamps, which hung down from dried human intestines. That done, he laid the table and set on it their favourite dish: a plate of decaying brain taken from a body dissected in the amphitheatre at the Medical School; they spread it thinly on some bread and ate the lot. They washed down their meal with an excellent bottle of vintage asthmatic sputum, harvested in hospitals. They then delighted in reading from *Les Chants de Maldoror*; the deranged aspect of this work, a blend of brilliant insanity and insane genius, set the tone for their time together. Mauri declaimed, in a voice from beyond the grave, the following stanzas, of which they never tired:

"It was a spring day. The birds were pouring out their canticles in twittering song, and human beings, returned to their various tasks, were bathing in the holiness of fatigue. Everything was working out its destiny: the trees, the planets, the sharks. Everything save the Creator! He was lying in the road, his clothes in tatters. His lower lip drooped like a soporific rope; his teeth were filthy, and the blond waves of his hair were thick with dust. Stupefied by a torpid drowsiness, crushed against the stones, his body was making unavailing efforts to rise. His strength had left him and he lay feeble as an earthworm, unfeeling as the bark of a tree. Floods of wine filled the ruts hollowed out by his shoulders' nervous twitchings. Hog-snouted brutishness spread over him its protective pinions and gazed upon him lovingly. His slack-muscled legs, like two fallen masts, dragged along the ground. Blood dribbled from his nostrils; his face, in his fall, had smashed against a post… He was drunk! Horribly drunk! Drunk as a bedbug that has, in one night, got through three tuns of blood! His voice echoed incoherently around the words I shall not repeat here; if the supreme drunkard has no self-respect, I, for my part, must respect mankind. Did you know that the Creator… got drunk! Pity that lip, soiled in orgy's cups! The hedgehog, that was passing by, dug into his back with its spines and said: 'There, take that. The sun has half run its course: work, you idler, and do not eat the bread of others. Just you wait while I call the cockatoo with its hooked beak.' The green woodpecker and the screech-owl, that were passing by, rammed their beaks right into his belly and said: 'There, take that. What are you doing here on this Earth? Is it to play out this dismal comedy for the animals? But I promise you that neither the mole, nor the cassowary, nor the flamingo will imitate you.' The ass, that was passing by, kicked him in the temple and said: 'There, take that. What have I done to you for you to give me such long ears? Even the lowly crickets scorn me.' The toad, that was passing by, squirted a jet of spittle on his brow and said: 'There, take that. If you had not made my eyes so huge, and I had seen you in the state you're in now, I would chastely have concealed the beauty of your limbs under a cascade of buttercups, forget-me-nots and camellias, so that none might see you.' The

117

lion, that was passing by, bent down his regal head and said: 'I, for my part, respect him, even though his splendour seems to us for the moment eclipsed. You others, who play the high and mighty, are nothing more than cowards, since you attacked him while he slept, how would you care to be in his place and putting up with the insults, from those passing by, you have heaped upon him?' Man, who was passing by, halted before the unrecognised Creator; and, to the applause of the crab-louse and the viper, shat for three whole days upon his noble countenance! Misfortune strike mankind for this insult!"*

"Something else," his mother said. "This divine satiety begins to nauseate."

And Mauri went on to another *chant.*

"Every night, plunging with the span of my wings down into my dying memory, I would call up the recollection of Falmer... every night. His blond hair, his oval face, his majestic features were still imprinted on my imagination... indestructibly... above all his blond hair. Begone, begone then, this hairless head, shiny as a tortoise shell. He was fourteen, and I only a year older. Let that lugubrious voice be silent. Why does it come to denounce me? But it is I myself that speaks. Using my own tongue to express my thought, I perceive that my lips are moving and that it is I myself speaking. And it is I myself who, telling a story from my youth, and feeling remorse enter deeply into my heart... it is I myself, unless I am mistaken... it is I myself that is speaking. I was only a year older. Who is it then I am speaking of? A friend I had in days gone by, I believe. Yes, yes, I have already mentioned his name... no, no, I do not wish again to spell out those six letters. Nor is it any use repeating I was a year older. Who knows? Repeat it none the less, but in a painful murmur: I was only a year older. Even then, my greater bodily strength was rather a reason for supporting he who had given himself to me, along life's difficult way, than for mistreating a visibly weaker creature. Now, I believe he was in fact weaker... Even then. He was a friend I had in days gone by, I believe. My greater bodily strength... every night... Above all his blond hair. Many a human being has seen bald heads: old age, illness, sorrow (the three of them together, or taken separately) offer a satisfactory explanation for this negative phenomenon. Such, at least, is the answer a learned man would provide me, were I to ask him. Old age, illness, sorrow. But I am not unaware (I too am a learned man) that one day, because he stayed my hand just as I was raising my dagger to thrust it into a woman's breast, I seized him by the hair in an iron grip and whirled him through the air at such a speed that his hair remained in my hand and his body, propelled by centrifugal force, smashed against the trunk of an oak tree... I am not unaware that, one day, his hair remained in my hand. I too am a learned man. Yes, yes, I have already mentioned his name. I am not unaware that one day I committed a vile deed, while his body was propelled by centrifugal force. He was fourteen. When, in an access of mental derangement, I flee over the fields, holding, pressed to my heart, a bloody thing I have long preserved as a holy relic, the little children who pursue me... the little children and the old women who pursue me, throwing stones, with these piteous laments: 'That's Falmer's hair.' Begone, begone then, this hairless head, shiny as a tortoise shell... A bloody thing. But it is I myself who is speaking. His oval face, his majestic features. Now, I believe he was in fact weaker. The old women and the little children. Now, in fact, I believe... what is it I was wanting to say?... now, in fact, I believe he was weaker. With an iron grip. That impact, was it that impact which killed him? Were his bones... irreparably... broken against the tree? Did it kill him, that impact, engendered by an athlete's strength? Did he remain alive, even though his bones were broken irreparably... irreparably? That impact, did it kill him? I fear to know what my closed eyes did not witness. In fact... Above all his blond hair. In fact I fled far from there with a conscience thereafter implacable. He was fourteen. With a conscience thereafter implacable. Every night. When a young man, who aspires to fame, in a fifth-floor room, bent over his desk at the silent midnight hour, barely hears a rustling sound he cannot explain, turns in all directions a head heavy with meditation and dusty manuscripts; but nothing, no sudden clue reveals the cause of what he so faintly hears, though hear it he does. At length he perceives that the smoke of his candle, rising to the ceiling, provokes in the surrounding air the almost imperceptible vibrations of a sheet of paper hanging from a nail driven into the wall. In a fifth-floor room. Just as a young man, who aspires to fame, hears a rustling sound he cannot explain, so I hear a melodious voice that says in my ear: 'Maldoror!' But, before correcting his misapprehension, he thought he heard a mosquito's wings… bent over his desk. I am not dreaming, though; what matter if I am lying on my satin bed? Coolly I make the perspicacious observation that my eyes are open, even though it is the hour of pink hooded-cloaks and masked balls. Never… oh! no, never!… did a mortal voice utter in these seraphic tones, pronouncing, with such painful eloquence, the syllables of my name! A mosquito's wings… How kindly his voice is. Has he then forgiven me? His body smashed against the trunk of an oak tree… 'Maldoror!' "*

"Enough, it's getting on my nerves."

And thus they remained, stupefied until the following morning.

Before parting, de Noirof said to his mother:

"When shall we be done with loving each other platonically?"

"Later," she replied. "You are my son, and I do not wish to sin with you as long as your wife still lives."

"And if she dies after us?"

"We shall love one another on high."

She added:

 "So make her die; get her to eat fatty, starchy foods; one day she'll choke to death, and that will be our salvation. The only thing in the world that matters is us. Nobody will ever guess at the sublimities hidden within our hearts. Nobody here on earth eats the brains from corpses and drinks the spittle of asthmatics. Let us act so that we might die in the satisfaction of having experienced, we alone, the True Sensation, of That Which Does Not Die."

Then she added:

"Give me some money."

She was emptying his wallet. His ministerial salary was fading away. Only rarely did he venture a remark:

"You're taking everything."

"Tap your mother-in-law," she replied. "Oh, how I have it in for that woman! Because it was her that brought that wife of yours into the world. She's got in the way of my Pleasure, the bitch!"

In this way an underlying communion united the souls of mother and son.

"The way of pleasure. As far as sensations are concerned, those people are middle-class. You've married beneath yourself by marrying that woman, you cannot love her, you never will. Oh but you know I'm not preaching the morality of the common herd here. To start with, there is no morality. Each of us carries our instincts within ourselves, and instinct doesn't take kindly to being moulded. It's not to be manipulated like a chemical product, its impulse is stronger than any obstacles that might stand in its way. On the other hand, instinct is innate. Consequently, our state of consciousness is a matter of chance, and, in its turn, chance is no more malleable than instinct… The way of pleasure. Yes, she's got in my way. And I can't forgive her, I cannot forgive her!"

She really did have it in for her. Everything she did was designed to bring about her complete ruin. Lacking the means, she acted in the opposite way to harlots who, after the hard labour of the flesh, in the evening hand over what they've earned to their pimps; Madame de Noirof gave no money to her son, it was he who gave the money to her. And each time she asked for more, so much so that one day Mauri was driven to his mother-in-law for funds. Madame Israël was not at all reluctant; her son-in-law was a minister, could one refuse a minister anything? However, the weekly drain on her finances became alarming, and she went to her daughter's house in the Rue de Rennes to try and clear the matter up. There she met Madame de Noirof who promptly leapt on her, gave her a mouthful of abuse, slapped her about and said: "Take that, you bitch! Take that, you old sow! Take that, you freak!" This last insult put Madame Israël flat out on her back; she left right away and never showed her face again. And her purse-strings would no more be untied.

Mauri hit upon the bright idea of asking to see his parents-in-law's criminal records, and was thunderstruck at what he found: old man Israël had twenty-three convictions for affronts to public decency, and had died in prison; Madame Israël had been prosecuted before she was married for infanticide, and had copped five years' hard labour. Mauri had the full records unearthed and brought them to the Rue Tronson du Coudray. While waiting for his mother, sitting at the table with a plate of brains and a bottle of sputum (greenish, phlegmy and veined with little threads of blood), he scanned the files. He took note of the juiciest details. When she was eighteen, and a skilful fencer, the accused gave birth in secret to an infant sired by her own father. She raised it until it was weaned, then killed it. She killed it by hanging it by the tongue and thrusting red-hot fencing foils into its body. The examining magistrate succeeded in proving that the murderess sang hymns while running her child through; the body had been pierced a hundred and sixty times. When it was dead she cut it down and shoved a toad into its mouth; then she gouged out its eyes and replaced them with rotten plums, gathered from an orchard at the hour of the angelus.*

"My mother's going to be absolutely delighted when she sees all this,"

Mauri said to himself. "What a stroke of luck!"

He turned to the file on Hermine. Should he open it? Had his wife something on her conscience too? Yes, there was something: six days in prison for being drunk and disorderly, on two occasions a fortnight's imprisonment for shoplifting, at the Louvre and in Bon Marché, and a conviction for attempted murder... Her! So fat, so self-possessed, so well brought-up!

"What a lovely family!"

Madame de Noirof arrived. When they had dined on brains and sputum, they reburied their noses in the files. One thing surprised Mauri: his mother was not as overjoyed as he had expected. She spoke with a certain forbearance of the fallibility of mankind, which so many circumstances can turn to crime.

"My dear, even the biggest criminals have a right to forgiveness... Man is not accountable at that precise moment when he commits a crime... Every man punished by the law is a man absolved... We never know what might one day happen to us. Nevertheless, when I next see your mother-in-law, I shall slip into our conversation a few words that won't exactly be coated in honey. Have you stopped sending me flowers?"

He had left them in his carriage. He was always mislaying things in cabs. At the police station or the lost-property office he recognised as his own forty-four umbrellas, two overcoats, three jars of preserves, a pot of pâté de foie gras, seventeen and a half pairs of gloves, a ministerial robe, two pairs of silk stockings and the piece of brick! That piece of brick from the Boulevard de Montrouge! Plus a pair of ladies' ankle-boots, six boxes of cigars, a pair of underpants, a stuffed bird, some tins of sweets and a package full of decorations — for decorated he was, and decorated all over the place, including: the Légion d'Honneur, the Christ of Portugal and the Order of the Turnscrew. At night, when affairs of state seemed intent on running round and round his head, he would get up and pin all his decorations on to his nightshirt. Then he could fall asleep.

Hermine was packing her bags. She was about to leave for Mers-les-Bains, a little Channel port renowned for its healthy air and much frequented by society ladies during pregnancy. Bellowing noises came from the bedroom; Mani-Mina was writhing with labour pains, though the midwife hadn't expected anything for another five days.

"Be off with you," said Mauri. "I don't want you around when this embarrassing thing happens. Can you forgive me?"

"I give you my pardon, Monsieur. And you?"

"Me? What are you trying to say?"

"Nothing. Tell me though, how do you suppose, Monsieur trumped-up minister, that all this came about?"

"Don't make fun of politics. Nowadays, if you haven't been a minister or something similar then you're a nobody; if you don't mind, let's put an end to this conversation right here. I'm awash with milk. If anyone in the government got wind of this, I'd be a laughing-stock. We have the good fortune — or the misfortune, if you prefer — to be witnessing the end, the dying moments of a century in such a state of mental feverishness as will never be surpassed. Let us rejoice. Now go to Mers, I shall suckle Mani-Mina's child. And don't booze it up too much, eh? Don't pinch anything either. Oh, and don't try to kill anyone."

"Eh?"

"Yes, I know all about it."

"Yes indeed, God forbid that you should make such insinuations!"

"It's not a question of insinuations, you have a criminal record, your mother likewise and your father likewise."

"Well then, how about your family? It's hardly any better than ours! Don't you read any of the opposition's newpapers then? If our family isn't beyond reproach, neither is yours. If my mother has a criminal record, so does yours. And your father likewise."

"My father likewise?"

"Yes, likewise!"

"Likewise?"

"Likewise!"

He asked to see his family's records. Hermine was right: Monsieur de Noirof had been convicted on fourteen occasions for fraud and multiple breaches of trust. By the time she was thirty, Madame de Noirof had spent one three-hundred-and-sixtieth of her life in prison for inciting minors to debauch. And he was Minister for Justice! His past alone was unblemished!

The following Friday (it was July) the weather was broiling hot. Madame de Noirof arrived at the Rue Tronson du Coudray in a state of extreme agitation.

"We're done for!"

"Again? Have you done something stupid again?"

"Yes, old fellow. Again. I bought an antique bidet, all carved, that once belonged to Charlotte Corday,* but I paid for it with counterfeit money."

As she confessed, she drank several glasses of asthmatic sputum. She'd already emptied a bottle right off. She started on another, clotted with the debris of decayed lungs, and in which greenish phlegm, white mucus and red saliva could be seen clearly floating. She swallowed, unflinchingly, while eating spoonfuls of decayed brain.

"… with counterfeit money. The dealer reported it to the authorities and they came and arrested me. Please, can you hush this up!"

He reflected for a moment.

"I will, but on one condition: that you grease my palm."

"I'm stony broke."

"Very well then, that's too bad. The matter will just have to follow its course. I am quite prepared to make every possible concession, but that requires money. It doesn't matter where you get it, just get me some."

"And your mother-in-law?"

"Ever since you gave her a going-over she's been constipated in the purse."

"Would you like me to try and unconstipate her?"

"If you succeed, it will earn you a full discharge."

She left. He returned to the ministry where a telegram summoned him urgently to the Rue de Rennes. Mani-Mina was dead, but there in a cradle beside her death-bed, kicking its feet, lay a strong little infant with four heads, eight arms, eight hands, half male and half female. It was in good health. With tears in his eyes Mauri kissed it, and right away set to suckling it. This was no easy matter. Mauri had only two breasts but his progeny had four mouths. The boy-half had scarcely had its fill when the other half claimed its pittance.

"I'll never be done with this," he repeated, turning it in all directions.

For the heads were placed like the points of the compass; the body had only one pelvis, with the four spines fused at the buttocks.

"If the world was populated with citizens such as this, we'd all die laughing!"

He let his mother know of this quadruply unique birth; she came the next day, accompanied by a strange red-headed man who was thin, badly dressed and ill-shod, and uncouth in his manner. He carried a folder under his left arm, under his right arm he carried nothing. His eyes had a strange, fixed stare; they were so vivid they were wearing out the lenses of the spectacles they sheltered behind. He was a bailiff, by the name of Zosku. He intended serving Mauri with a something-or-other. The latter, in the act of hanging a stuffed owl from the ceiling above the corpse, had climbed up a step-ladder, and it was from there, perched on the top rung, that he parleyed with the catchpole.*

"May it please His Excellence to hear me. In the name of a fictitious debtor (and he wiggled his backside as he spoke) I come to call upon her to pay, within twenty-four hours, the sum of one hundred thousand francs that is due."

"Let's say," said Mauri, "less of a round figure: ninety-one thousand, two hundred and thirty-four francs, seventy-five centimes. And then?"

"Then? You will go and present this stamped paper to your esteemed mother-in-law. So as to avoid a scandal, if she loves her daughter — and she does love her — she will cough up. Every time you end up in these financial difficulties, we shall start the process over again."

"It was my idea," said Madame de Noirof.

Mauri assumed a funeral-on-a-wet-day expression and went off to see Madame Israël; with a double catch in her voice, she bewailed her son-in-law's predicament.

"Try to organise your life better now. My poor Hermine, our fortune is fading away. *Ora pro nobis.** And now please be off with you."

Mauri returned, thoroughly crestfallen. Upon hearing the fateful news, his mother said:

"It's all the same to me. There'll be a scandal. It's not as if I wanted it to turn out this way. I'll be arrested tomorrow, and you'll get the sack. You know full well you won't keep your portfolio — or your dispatch-case — when they find out your mother has been arrested as a counterfeiter. I shall be going to prison."

"Go then! But before that…"

He was looking at the dead body and a satanic and Sardanapalian* idea went through his mind.

"I was thinking that," said Madame de Noirof supportively. "We'd need a cold chisel and a hammer."

"No, a saw would be preferable."

They found one and carefully laid out Mani-Mina's corpse on a sheet of oilcloth. Mani's body still bore traces of plasma and sticky fluids tinged with blood; as for Mina's, it was as dry as a mummy from the time of Sesostris;* she no longer had breasts, they had fallen in, leaving two hollows in their place. The profile of her face was like one of those steel wedges foresters use when splitting a piece of wood standing on end. Her skin called to mind those paintings by Memlinc* before they had been restored — lupus had variegated it with ancient-looking colours, and the blemishes had taken on clearly defined shapes. On her right thigh, a lucky combination of these marks, with their clear outlines, gave the impression of a biblical landscape depicting, in the foreground, a virgin holding a palm-leaf and with a halo round her head; in the middle distance, a silvery river; in the background, above a barren mountain, a fiery sky, through an opening in which the Most High had thrust his head, pulling a face at humankind. With the utmost dexterity, Mauri cut this piece of skin from the thigh with a razor, and glued it to a wooden panel.

"We'll get it framed, and then we'll put it up for auction and see what it'll fetch. It's a very nice little item. And at least this one won't lack a certain dewiness!"

He brought his lines of sight into convergence upon the noble countenance of his bitch of a mother, and uttered these words:

"I'm even inclined to get it framed right away and show it to an expert; if it has any value, if, for example, they offer me sixteen thousand francs or thereabouts — that's the absolute minimum — we can carry on skinning dear Mina. If there's nothing doing, we'll suspend operations, there's no point in tiring ourselves out for bugger all."

Now, it happened that the expert they showed this unusual image to yelped three and a half times with surprise, looked askance at Noirof, and grabbed him by the collar.

128

"This has been stolen from the Louvre, I recognise it. It was in the

Flemish gallery, on the left, by the entrance… No? Am I wrong, am I wrong on this point?"

"In your opinion, what's it worth?"

"Oh, that would be fifty-odd thousand francs. These Memlincs are very rare, Memlincs from his first period."

So the flaying continued. On her back they noticed a nice little Vollon,* a tambourine, slashed by Richelieu's sword which had a nightcap with no tassel over its pommel but was missing a blood-runnel. From the left calf they peeled off an epidermic disc depicting an old plate copied from Bernard Palissy.* Then, carried away by a fit of sacrilegious destruction, they tore off the rest of the skin, cutting it up into small pieces, and by cleverly re-combining the fragments succeeded in putting together a lovely little Corot, minus the signature.

"That lot," she said, "is easily worth ninety-one thousand francs."

But they were in a hurry to see their secret project through: with the saw they made cross-cuts in both skulls and extracted the marrow. Mani's smelt good, but the other stank like carrion.

"Let's eat that one quick," said Madame de Noirof. "I could eat a horse."

But because they weren't able to drink any of their sputum while they were eating they suffered from indigestion and spewed up Mina's brain. After that, they ate again what each had just vomited up, and felt no further upset.

"Are we agreed about dismissing the charge?" she persisted.

"My conscience balks at such injustice," Mauri replied. "The matter will take its course."

"Shitbag!" she screamed. "Snake in the grass! And the Bishop of Djurdjura's coming in eleven days! What a let-down!"

They were going quite mad. Besides, the shock-wave caused by Messé-Malou's discoveries was softening the brains of humanity. The stupendiosity of his latest invention brought this brain-softening to its utter culmination. After the man-tree, soon officially adopted for the repopulation* of France, Messé-Malou discovered the tree-lamp. This was a tree that flowered eternally. During the day, the flowers stayed closed; when twilight came, they opened up and gave off a light that grew brighter even as the nocturnal darkness deepened. Just one of these flowers had the same luminescence as ten thousand candles.

Shortly afterwards, Mauri received the following letter:

Mère celèbin, 1 clok, eevenin

Mye dear frend
Ive wrote you these fiewords
to tel you. that ime settelled in Mercelebaint
wich is, the moste
      plesentest plaice. that I knows. I writesyou thez. feuwords
azwife aloan to say. there are heer lots off flouring trees in grate
      quan tities.
        and grasstoo
i miscarrid yestidy in the seawater. mye Kiddi went off wiv the
waives. That will bii rifreshmint. for the fishis
COME ANSEEME. FORADAY. *That will beveri*
      nice fourme. I prays. god four you.
     Your misundistood wife Airmine

He said to his mother:

"You have associated with scoundrels to produce counterfeit money and

I could, with a word, call off the investigation. Yes, I could, if I did not love you. In the present state of the love that unites us, to cause you pain would bring me enormous delight. Because to see you unhappy would magnify my love for you; I should like to have you suffer such refinements of cruelty as permit me to attain the greatest possible sum of happiness. Such as severing one of your limbs, or making you drink molten metal; I should like to see you writhing in spasms of the most atrocious agony. I would be so happy! And afterwards, what transports, what intoxication! We would love each other far more! A man is never truly content until he can do *a little* harm to his fellows. Especially to his mother!"

Then he turned his attention to how the investigation was coming along. He himself issued the orders for his mother to be arrested at a specific time, and took up a position on the Rue de Presbourg, so as to witness this formality being carried out. As it happened, the Bishop of Djurdjura had just arrived, with a long string of people in soutanes and an old man whose face was mysteriously hidden; he was barely able to walk, and was supported by two cardinals. They were at table. The old man with the mysteriously hidden face ate nothing. Madame Perle and the Duc de la Croix de Berny were among the guests.

"Tomorrow is the great day," the Bishop announced. "I trust these ladies will do us the honour of being present at the ceremony."

He spoke volubly of his hunting exploits in Africa, of missions undertaken in sandy deserts, among savages and wild beasts. For once he drank only water, very slightly tinted with red wine. And, with dessert, he took no liqueur.

"I do beg you, Monsignor, you'll only weaken your stomach. Just a little cognac?"

"No thank you, Madame, I'm not permitted cognac. I have the clap."

He explained that he had contracted this love-sickness in the land where fog flourishes.

131

"Yes, Madame, in London. That would not be at all surprising to anybody familiar with the anomalies which form the foundation of that nation's customs. You've never visited the English capital, Madame? You should go there one day, but take some luggage, because without luggage an unaccompanied woman is not admitted to a hotel. Go there and see for yourself. It's absolutely charming. As soon as you set foot on British soil you see only things which offend us French people, accustomed as we are to joy and bright sunshine: frigid people with a chilly manner, continuously pelting rain, fogs thick with coal dust, muddy streets, as sticky as wallpaper-paste, and a germanified gobbledegook spoken egoistically and incomprehensibly, so intent is the Englishman to remain inscrutable and to keep for himself his language, his customs and his soil — that is what awaits you. As soon as you step ashore, you sense that you're being left to your own devices, and that there will never be any fellow feeling between our two peoples. You'll make your way around the swarming metropolis as if the sole living being among a multitude of walking corpses. For the Englishman is, above all, a dead man. Life cannot endure in so corpse-like a constitution, undisturbed by any demonstration of the emotions and with a marmoreal facial expression no smile would dare light up. No, Madame, an Englishman never laughs. He has much more important things to do. He spends his time drinking, drinking cold things, soda-water, whisky, brandy, then whisky, soda-water, brandy, then soda-water, brandy, whisky. He drinks constantly, and standing up: he never sits down. He gets tipsy standing up, that's how he manages not to stagger. He drinks without interruption, and on Sunday he rests. On Sunday, he doesn't drink quite as much. The *public houses* are closed while religious services take place; the interminable queues of people waiting with their tongues hanging out for worship to be over, so that they might gorge themselves again, are a sight to be seen. They swig down their drink greedily, then go home to be bored, in conformity with the law.

Because the law ordains that they be bored on Sundays, and they obey the law. Even in his own house an Englishman may not play cards on a Sunday — that is forbidden. During the week he may play cards, but not in *public houses* or cafés; no. At the club, Madame, only at the club. Go to London, Madame, and you shall never set foot in a club. Nor will you see any trams, and should you be caught with the urge to piss, not a chance. Before leaving for London you'll need to piss at home, of that I must advise you, because in London people don't piss, nor do they shit."

"But why?"

"Because London lacks water-closets. To my knowledge, there is only one, though a fine one it is, a veritable monument. Take note of the address, Madame: it is in Piccadilly, opposite the American Bar. People come to use it from a good five miles round. There one may piss very comfortably and for nothing; it's four *sous* to have a shit though. That's nothing, the way prices are. It's a monument, I tell you, as big as the dome of Les Invalides,* and the same shape. I can vouch for its being very smart, and people pee and shit inside this dome right up until midnight. After midnight the monument is closed. You then have no choice but to save your business till morning."

"And the women, Monsignor?"

"Ah yes, let's talk about them! And just about them, if you don't mind. Well now, what shall I say, Madame? In London, things are not the same as everywhere else; there are women, but not ordinary women, no; these are extraordinary women. London, which has five million inhabitants, has something in the region of a hundred tarts. So you see, there are possibilities. So far, so good. Yes. But they're poxed, and that's not so good. We learn everything, don't we Madame, from experience, including the pox… You object? Let's pretend I didn't mention that. The prevalence of infection among these women of easy virtue in London stems from the fact that prostitution there is not controlled. It's not at all in keeping for such a prudish nation. I've tried very hard to discover the reason but I haven't succeeded. This liberty for women, who aren't subject to any medical inspection, who are not registered like our own, is very dangerous. Three quarters of these wretches who make a living from their charms are infected foreigners driven from their own countries by the nuisance of having to be treated. They are infected, and they infect others. I am the proof of that."

"You should have gone to a brothel, Monsignor!"

"But dear lady, there are no brothels in London."

"Really? Not even one little brothel?"

"Not one."

"But if there aren't any brothels, then there's nothing at all in that albionesque capital."

"You've hit the nail on the head my dear. The brothels were closed down ten years ago so as to combat the scourge of prostitution and to push young people into getting married. The disappearance of *maisons de tolérance* was the work of a lord in parliament. This lord was a model of chastity; dissolute morals were an annoyance to him, his dream was the universality of Virtue. It is probably for this reason that he was recently sentenced to a year in prison for public indecency with a boy under the age of sixteen. Either it makes sense or it doesn't."

At that moment two officers of the law came in and served Madame de Noirof with a warrant to bear witness. All those present found the joke in the best possible taste and laughed for a long while following her departure for Saint-Lazare.

Next day, from the morning onwards, Paris was inundated by hordes of priests and nuns hurrying to make their way up the Butte aux Cailles. It was the site of a vast Greek temple, near Fontaine à Mulard, and only those who had made a vow of chastity or had assumed priestly functions could enter. Following upon an excessively ecumenical synod convened in Rome, it was decided that members of the clergy might henceforth drink to inebriation from the cup of carnal delights, and the construction of a huge pleasure-house for the exclusive use of ecclesiastics was agreed. The Bishop of Djurdjura had taken it upon himself to seek funds, from right and left, but ended up with more than was needed. Churchmen coughed up their groats, priests prodded their flocks and in less than a week, four million francs were collected. Independently of the capital set aside to cover the costs of construction, a capital sum was needed as a reserve to reimburse those members of the minor clergy living far from Paris who also had a right to a slice of the cake. The female contingent was conscripted from the convents; preference was given to sisters with a generous backside, as well as to worldly misses who had renounced the joys of the here-below and who asked no more than to treat themselves to an occasional piss-up. Ouch! Ouch! Since there were more women than men, it was agreed that they should be renewed weekly; in this way there would always be plenty of fresh meat and everybody would be satisfied.

A church, more than twice the size of Notre Dame, had been built in the centre of the temple for the daily celebration of mass, since the motto they had chosen was: Duty before All. Mass had to be said daily; the worship of God came before the worship of Love. The religious emblems which decorate Catholic churches had been replaced by profane subjects. For all that, the paintings were entirely discreet, and only initiates would recognise the allusions they contained. Thus the tenth Muse* was personified in a large panel depicting her, racked with despair, on the point of hurling herself into the sea from the top of the Leucadian promontory. The sculptures, on the other hand, being openly pagan, greatly offended decency, and their realism was quite shocking; when the incense whirled about the altar, and the pious chants set to rhythm by the organ launched the vast vessel on to an ocean of mystical music, the obscene side of these bronzes and marbles was hideous, and this disparity was altogether revolting. To the objections raised on this matter, the Bishop responded:

"I know what we're like; we'd all be overdoing the hanky-panky if there weren't something to calm us down. You'll see how the sacrilegious nature of these statues will return our senses to harmony."

In this he was mistaken.

By midday the temple was packed solid. The men occupied the right half of the nave, the women the left. They were naked. By way of headgear the women wore bishops' mitres, new ones; the men had nuns' winged coifs, old ones. The Duc, Madame Perle and Mauri de Noirof had taken their places in the choir stalls, by their presence giving the inauguration an official character, so to speak. All were standing. Suddenly the booming of the organ pipes announced the solemn entry of the officiating priest. In evening dress, white tie, polished shoes and opera-hat, this was the old man with the mysteriously veiled face who the previous evening had not wished to eat at Mauri's mother's house. He entered, supported by two stark-naked cardinals, recognisable by their *biretti*, and haltingly delivered the mass. He seemed terribly aged, much changed but still quite energetic overall; few popes, at his age, would have troubled to leave Rome and bring their blessing to so impious a foundation. For this old man was indeed the pope in person, Jesus Christ's minister plenipotentiary on Earth. He had left the Vatican on the entreaties of Madame Perle, who thereby hoped to tire him out and bring about his death. For he was indeed tired; when he turned round for the *Dominus vobiscum*, his face looked so piteous that it appeared sunk into deathly dissolution. At the *Orate fratres* he stood motionless, his arms crossed and in a state of shock: the

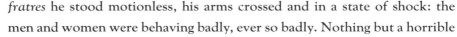

men and women were behaving badly, ever so badly. Nothing but a horrible jumble of throbbing bodies, distorted and yelling; over this heaving mass, this fantastic tangle of naked forms, rays of sunlight which had pierced the stained-glass windows cast blotches in myriad colours; above this, bishops' mitres, quite new, and nuns' old winged coifs fluttered about here and there in triumph. The hoarse throaty death-rattle of Satisfaction, symphony of the Flesh, rose up, muted by the symphony of the organ.

A great deal of incense had to be burnt to dissipate the smell of this bloodless struggle. The Bishop of Djurdjura had certainly not been a good prophet. The pope was dumbfounded. Instead of continuing the mass, he rested for a few minutes. Taking advantage of this pause, the slap-artist was given the opportunity to proceed with the execution of an adulterer by means of the new guillotine, called the noirofine, in honour of its illustrious inventor. A ministerial decree commanded that adulterers were to receive their punishment in the Temple of Love on the Butte aux Cailles. And this was the first execution.

The instrument, all set up, was placed on a platform, somewhat to the front of the choir, and to ensure that none present should wallow in the pornographic details of the decapitation, the noirofine was surrounded by screens which left only the blade visible. The guilty party was brought in — a very distinguished, although undecorated man of more than seventy; he was positioned between the executioner's two assistants, Pancrace and another cabby from the depot in the Rue Campagne-Première, and the slap-artist walked in front. The unfortunate individual was led behind the screens. The eyes of all those present were fixed upon the blade. The blade did not fall. The cortège reappeared just as it had entered. The executioner had a brief conversation with Noirof, after which the condemned man was paraded through the ranks of women who had just then put on something more suitable. This produced its effect. The dismal cortège retired once more behind the screens and, a second later, the blade fell with a dull thud, followed by a fearful yelp of pain. The devalued morsel of flesh was displayed to the public on the tip of a pike; the guillotine was removed, and the pope concluded the mass. The *Ite Missa est* once pronounced, the sovereign pontiff gave his benediction; and immediately a wildly bustling rush precipitated the couples towards the five hundred little boudoirs placed all round the Temple. The solemn hour for the decelibation of the clergy had struck.

A dispute arose between Mauri de Noirof and the guard on the train.

"You won't," the guard insisted, "get round the regulations; you waount, God damn it, get round it! You waount never get round it!"

"But I'm carrying it on my knees!"

"That doesn't matter. There's four of them. You'll have to pay for an extra seat."

"Excuse me, in the regulations it says *infants*."

"Yes, but it's a plural that's a singular. *Infants* means *the infant*. You have four infants, right? That's three too many you're lugging about, you need a whole seat. That'll be more comfortable. If we used your system you could get on the train with fifty minors all under the age of three but only pay for the one seat. I ask you, is that reasonable?"

And for the whole journey from Paris to Tréport, Mauri endured a a series of testing moments. Paul-Uc-Zo-Émilie, as Mani-Mina's little one was called, gave him no end of trouble. He was never off the teat. At the stopping-stations, at Persan-Beaumont, which the guard called Person-Beauman, at Méru, which he pronounced Rému, at Beauvais, for which he substituted Veaubais, crowds on the platform lined up at the carriage door so that they might enjoy the show, which was so out of the ordinary. Never had they seen a man with milk-engorged breasts, far less a quadruple-bodied child. The heat was intense. Mauri dozed off. At Longroy-Gamaches he awoke, soaked in pee and baby cack. He hadn't brought a towel, and he was wearing a flannel suit.

The preferments of power were beginning to pall on him. On top of that he had noticed that his colleagues were giving him disapproving looks when they met in committee. His inferiority was obvious; he had put up a poor defence of his budget and, as a result of this clumsiness, the grant usually given to the Bishop of Djurdjura, to promote the desavagisation of black Africans, had not been voted through. Yielding to his mother's supplications, he had swept the counterfeiting business under the carpet, and the papers had thundered at such an injustice. All this turned his stomach.

His arrival at Mers caused a revolt among the bathers. A retinue of five or six hundred persons followed him in his peregrinations about the little town, which he paced from north to south and from east to west, to locate his wife. She had not sent him her address, and he had not remembered to ask for it. Craving a rest, he stopped at the Hôtel de la Plage, so called because it was a kilometre from the sea. The manager, who was complaining about how bad business was, all of a sudden saw his establishment invaded. Crowds of people squeezed themselves in, wanting to see the little monster. Mauri left it in the hands of a couple of wet-nurses and, relieved of the burden of breast-feeding, set off in search of Hermine. In the distance, on the shingle beach, a barrel-shaped object caught his attention: it was her. She lay in the sun, her head stuffed into a white bathing-cap, her fat body swelling out under a flannel dress, also white: a mass as white as the ermine whose delicate slimness she would never contrive to make her own. She found him very brusque.

"It's as if you were some sort of telegram. Politics, eh?"

"A bit of that, and the rest of it. Where the devil are you staying, then? I had to leave all my stuff at the hotel. I wanted to give you a surprise, by not telling you I was coming, but there's my pleasure spoiled."

"I'm happy to see you. I hope you can rid this place of the presence of a certain individual the sight of whom makes my flesh creep to the point that I was on the point of leaving. You know, the man with the camel's nose... what's he called?"

"Jardisse?"

"That's the one. I can't take two steps without having to suffer running into him. God, how I hate him! Oh, I hate him! I hate him!"

She added:

"Since you've put up at the hotel, you might as well stay there. What's the point of coming to stay with me? We never sleep together. We can have lunch, dinner and go for walks. That's what's best to do at the seaside."

"And your teeth?"

"The teeth in my little gobby-wob? Still in a really rotten state. I'm drinking lots of brandy, it soothes my nerves a little."

"I thought there'd be more people here. It's high season!"

"Yes, but they all go to Tréport, which is over there, to the left. In the past the two parishes were one; they divided, and have been at loggerheads ever since. But Tréport is richer than Mers, so it advertises its beach more, organises lots of festivities, attracts lots of people, and so on. You understand? In Mers there are only solid citizens, well-fed people, pregnant women: it's plenty good enough for us."

She arranged to meet him the following morning, at nine o'clock prompt.

. . . .

～ AFFAIRS OF THE HEART ～

Cast:

She and He

The action takes place at Mers-les-Bains, in Hermine's bedroom.

She enters stealthily, feels about on the bed, and makes sure he's there.

HE: That you?

SHE: Shh! We need to be careful... My husband's turned up...

The curtain does not fall, the conversation does not cease.

· ·

The next day, Mauri was punctual and asked:

"You like it here?"

"Apart from running into Jardisse, very much so. One's so comfortable here, so much at home, everyone here's so very nice. Look, there's hardly anybody about."

"... hardly anybody."

And in fact, at that moment, there were only two bathers splashing about in the salty water, while six other human beings, stretched out like toads, were solemnly occupying their time throwing stones in the sea — as if it had asked to swallow again what it had earlier thrown up! — before themselves wallowing in this bitter pool of water.

"Let's sit down," she said.

"But what on?"

"On the shingle, where else!"

There was no other option.

"That must be uncomfortable," Mauri remarked.

"I assure you people here manage it perfectly well."

She plumped down. The shingle crunched under her weight; as for him, he stayed perched on some little pebbles, which hurt his backside.

"They really ought to get rid of all these pebbles and plant some grass here!"

"Yes. But that would be an almighty job."

As far as the eye could see, along the coastline, there was nothing but a carpet of shingle, and each day the sea washed up still more. This was laid down symmetrically, in undulating waves, the better to indicate that these deposits were its own work, since they were fashioned in its own image. This layering was enormously deep and would have required more than a few lifetimes' work to remove.

"In any case, what's the point? Sometimes the waves reach right up to the casino, and anything planted there would be removed in no time at all. And then there's no soil under the pebbles; under the pebbles, there's only more pebbles. Is that it then? And where does it all come from? It must come from Switzerland or Bohemia. Is there any knowing?"

A leaden sky weighed down on them; it was so hot that the air was boiling and because of their spherical form, the pebbles refracted the heat so that, whichever way they turned, they were stewing in their own juices; they were getting cooked on the belly, cooked on the back and cooked on the sides. The sea itself was sweating, it had slumped into a lazy torpor, its waves shuffling listlessly and as if in spite of themselves or in need of a kick in the arse to buck them up. And, apart from the creaking of the pebbles under the feet of a dog or a cat, a deep calm, pure as the soul of a new-born child, overlaid both earth and ocean. Some bathers came on the scene, a few at a time, seeming dejected or resigned. They too lay down on the stones, their snouts turned towards the waves, intent on sniffing up a little of the air that never quite managed to reach them. The sea was depressingly flat, opalescent and glistening, but so colourless at the horizon that it merged into the sky; or else the sky was bathing in it, there was no telling quite which.

"I think," said Mauri, "it's perfectly boring here."

Behind them, along the Rue de la Plage, people were out for a walk, yawning under their parasols; on occasion they stopped, took out their watches and looked at the time — but time had not moved on at all! Time was standing still, it hadn't the energy to move.

"You've managed to find the most dismal of beaches!"

"You think so?"

"Come on now, look at those faces over there! They're sincere, at least, they don't lie; sat atop a bust of Melancholy, they'd fit beautifully. And all you'd need do then would be to set them up on the rocks hereabouts, they'd blend in perfectly. I swear I see nothing about us here but uncouth rocks."

The cliffs were sheer and extremely high, crumbling, without contours and deathly pale. To the left, at the top of the cliffs at Tréport a cross could be seen; to the right, the cliffs at Mers could only boast two or three little abandoned houses. On either side they extended, looking sorry in a way that couldn't fully be defined, retreating by degrees before the sea's incursions as it nibbled away at their roots and their entrails of chalk, with the landslides that followed making them crumble away. In the deep silence around the pier — for the sea made scarcely a sound — there echoed suddenly the plaintive notes of a piano on which the uncertain fingers of a child were playing classical exercises.

"Let's be on our way; it must be less dreary somewhere else."

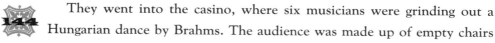

They went into the casino, where six musicians were grinding out a Hungarian dance by Brahms. The audience was made up of empty chairs

and benches.

"You know," said Hermine, "it's not always so deserted; there are people here sometimes, in the evenings, about a dozen or so. On Sundays the audience might number fifteen, sixteen or even seventeen. I tell you, there's nothing more homely than this resort."

Their playing was atrocious.

"It sounds like a pot on the hob."

"You're always the witty one, Monsieur de Noirof: this is a Duval restaurant."

It was in fact one of the pavilions built by the Duval firm in 1889, for the Universal Exhibition. The local authorities in Mers had done it up, but had made a hash of it and turned it into the local temple of music.

"It still smells of frying," said Mauri.

"Be quiet," a voice behind him ordered.

It was the casino manager.

"Eh?"

"Be quiet. You're not here to speak, nor to listen, nor breathe, nor move about; here, Monsieur, people are bored rigid."

And he stepped away, rudely, rolling his big braggart's eyes.

Meanwhile, the orchestra was playing the changes on the same phrase for the hundredth time; since he'd come in, Mauri had heard no other — a few bars laboriously expectorated, in which the clarinet whimpered a little pastorale made up on the spur of the moment.

"Are they doing it on purpose?"

He rose to his feet; the clarinettist was chomping on the mouthpiece of his instrument with his eyes lowered as if wishing to contemplate his navel. The others, too, seemed intent upon contemplating their navels. Yet it wasn't their navels they were contemplating, they weren't contemplating anything:

they were snoring. Now and then, in the middle of a dream, the conductor sighed: "*Piano… piano…*" And the band played *piano…*

They returned to the beach.

"It was there," she said, stretching out her left arm *à la* Sarah Bernhardt, "it was over there that I lost him. The cold of the water separated us from each other. He pissed off, the little fellow, without any fuss at all. Which reminds me, what about yours?"

"I brought it with me," he said. "It's a little different from us. You keen to see it?"

Damn it but she was keen! Puffing and blowing like a locomotive pulling a train of two hundred loaded trucks up a really steep incline, she hauled herself to the hotel. There were people waiting at the door; one by one they entered, then left by another door, dumbfounded.

"You could," said one of them, "put that monster in the Luxembourg when it's twenty, where that group by Carpeaux* stands — cover it in wax-polish and the illusion'd be complete."

The queue was getting longer; order was being maintained by a *gendarme*, the mayor and the police superintendent. The main road to Tréport was thick with people, and there was talk of special trains being laid on to enable the citizens of Dieppe to come and feast their eyes on Mauri's progeny. But Mauri was growing tired of it; he failed to understand this unwholesome curiosity and, since he was expressing these thoughts out loud, people gave him a mouthful of abuse.

"Don't put the rest of us off like that… What are you doing here if it upsets you so?"

At length their turn came and they could go into the hotel.

"That'll be fifty centimes each," a flunkey informed them.

And up in the room, next to Paul-Uc-Zo-Émilie, a money-box received the steady flow of coins. Mauri and Hermine did as everybody else: they deposited their penny and, after exclamations of wonderment, went out, marvelling to themselves.

"It looks like us," said Hermine.

"Yes, it already seems very intelligent."

"A wonderful thing, progress!"

They chatted about the upcoming potato harvest. This topic allowed Mauri to urge his wife to base her diet on starchy foods.

"Eat potatoes, plenty of potatoes — and above all, beans! The aeolian properties of that vegetable will make you slim."

At table, at mealtimes, he took this cynicism to the point of forcing her to eat second helpings. Hermine complied. She ate three, four. She swallowed sluggishly.

"My mother was right," Mauri thought to himself. "One of these days she'll choke to death. How delightful!"

"I'll keep an eye," she said, "on the effect these beans have; I've brought my weighing-machine with me, and I'll go on with this diet or stop it depending on what I weigh tomorrow. Today I weighed a hundred and eighteen kilos and three grammes, minus my dung."

They decided on a stroll to Tréport-Terrasse.

"The climb will be difficult for me. All the same, just to please you…"

"Have you noticed," said Mauri, "there was no fish on the menu. Usually, in a port, people eat fish."

She gave him an ironic look.

"What's that? You don't know? Have a look at the sea, Monsieur; do you see a fishing-boat? No. For the simple reason there's no fish in the sea here."

"But of course; they'd be too bored here. They'd rather get caught somewhere else."

The sun was unbearable.

"Come on then, what about a little bit of shade! What a stupid road, it's cooking and blinding us at the same time."

Mauri looked about him.

"Where are all the trees, then?"

"There aren't any. They tried planting some but they didn't grow; they shrank. Flowers can't grow either. The grass isn't quite so fussy, the big lawn under the windows of your hotel proves it — that lawn was sown more than a hundred times and in the end, it did grow, in fact you can still see the odd blade of grass here and there on occasion."

"And you choose a place like this for a holiday? A place where there are no birds, where there are no insects, where there are no trees, where there's nothing but people who… people who… people who…"

"Be a bit kinder. If you can manage to!"

They had reached the foot of the steps up to Tréport-Terrasse, a trifling climb of four hundred steps, almost perpendicular and with an unplaned wooden handrail that ran splinters into the skin and left those going up having to make do without the rail, saying "Heave ho!" to themselves to keep up their spirits and using their hands to keep their legs moving. They stopped, giving their lungs a break while their bodies absorbed a little of the heat, then steeled themselves to resume the ascent. Gradually the vastness of the sea became visible, and the people down below looked like lice, lice on a viper's back, abominably hideous for as long as they are so stupid as to show themselves to their fellows, however far away they may be. If man were aware how much ugly horror there follows in his wake, he would dig an enormous hole in the ground, shove in a thousand million kilogrammes of panclastite* and blow out the brains of the infected globe over

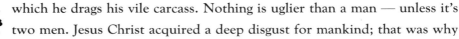

which he drags his vile carcass. Nothing is uglier than a man — unless it's two men. Jesus Christ acquired a deep disgust for mankind; that was why he got himself crucified, and thus no more was obliged to look upon mankind.

"Jesus was a canny fellow," said Mauri on reaching the top of the cliff. "They erect statues to him everywhere. But he must be thoroughly cheesed off up here, in the winter, the north wind must freeze the legs off him."

On the top of a low mound beset with a rusty iron railing there stood a miserable little cross. *Stat crux dum volvitur orbis.** He died to redeem men's sins, and the memory of that sacrifice would be eternal! The cross would live for ever! As long as the Earth turned, it would remain erect! It was man that pronounced this oracle, and his self-conceit is plainly visible throughout.

"Here we are," said Hermine, her skin running with sweat, "at the Terrasse. It's my favourite walk. We come here almost every day."

"What's that? *We* come here? Who with?"

"With the ladies. We all know each other. We confess our little secrets. When we have smelly feet, we openly admit it; if the maid has made a mess of the salad, if she goes to bed with Monsieur, if he has lovers, if they have mistresses, if these pay pimps, if those do in honest citizens, we confess all that, under the awnings, which we pull together as close as possible so that nothing gets out."

"Are they all respectable women?"

"Not a single one of them. They all deceive their husbands."

"Even you?"

"Even me. Oh, but with my moral tutor, nothing to worry about."

They paced up and down the Terrasse. It was a large uncultivated area, bordered for two or three thousand metres along the cliff-edge by a parapet of hemispherical perforated bricks and criss-crossed by a tracery of streets with pavements edged by gravel set in cement; where the lamp-posts should have been was marked by overgrown circular depressions, and at a crossroads, there was a cast-iron plaque bearing the inscription: FH.*

"There you are," she explained. "You look at all this and ask yourself questions you cannot answer. And so it is that I have to tell you that the town of Tréport once had the idea of creating here a suburb by the name of Terrasse. From the spot where we two rotting animals are standing, there is a magnificent view, offset by air polluted by the chimney-flues of Tréport. If indeed you deign to lower your regal gaze fifty metres below, you will discern only a panorama of roofs and the threads of smoke that escape them. It's extremely healthy. What is less so is the motive behind the Terrasse project. These bold fellows spent a few hundred thousand francs to build a stairway and then went off home, rubbing their hands together. And then you know what they did, Monsieur, every morning? Well now, they went out, pointed their snouts at the cliff, and then returned home again, saying: 'Still nothing.' There was still nothing."

"What were they expecting?"

"To see houses growing, of course! In the ordinary run of events, when people found a city they begin by building houses, and the space between them becomes a street. Here they've done the opposite: first of all they built the streets, telling themselves the houses would emerge of themselves. But, lo and behold, they didn't just grow. No use watering them, they don't come up. The land is so barren it produces nothing, not even houses."

They made their way along the edge of the cliff; way down below, at the cliff-bottom, the sea was chalky because of the easily weathered nature of the rocks against which it thudded. It was a dirty white, a white almost the colour of a chemise worn for six months by a louse-ridden woman whose grandfather was a coal merchant, and it carried this dirt to the beach — the human vermin who were having a soak were taking a muck-bath. Then they sat down.

"Do you suffer from vertigo?"

"Never."

"Then you could lean over the edge of a precipice quite easily, with no fear of falling."

"See for yourself!"

She took up a position on a rock ledge that hung out over the void. A little push, that would suffice: she'd be taking a one-way ticket to the land of eternity. This method would be quicker than wificide by the slow assimilation of leguminous starch from beans and potatoes. A red glint flashed in Mauri's retinas, a dryness seized his throat, he trembled, stood up and rushed towards her — but when some people out walking suddenly appeared he shouted loudly:

"Be careful, you're frightening me!"

"You used informal syntax towards me!"

"My mistake; I was afraid you'd tumble head over heels into the void and spoke that way to save time. Accidents happen so easily. Let's go, I'm thirsty."

They went back down. The immensity of the ocean diminished, and the viper's lice gradually resumed their normal forms. Just as they were getting foot-sore on the sharp paving-stones of Tréport, they ran into Jardisse, whose nose was becoming ever more ugly and repulsive. Jardisse walked passed them and sneered.

"You see," said Hermine, "the way he looked at us with contempt. Well now, that's how it is every time he walks by me. Oh, I hate him… I hate him!"

"Me too, I'm thirsty. Let's have something to drink in Tréport, because there's no cafés in Mers, except for the one in the Casino where you're not allowed to drink."

At that very moment the taste of the cigar Mauri had smoked long ago at Madame Perle's returned to his memory.

"I still have the stale scent of it in my mouth."

"Of what?"

"You wouldn't understand!"

They sat down outside a café. Hermine ordered a cognac; Mauri couldn't decide.

"Give me," he said to the waiter, "something that washes, that cleanses a man inwardly."

The man briefly sized him up.

"White wine, with lemon and soda-water."

"Is that good?"

"Excellent. Just you taste it."

He withdrew a little, then retraced his steps.

"I took the liberty of recommending that because it's what people always have when they're hung-over."

"I'd like it," said Hermine, "if our being able to see each other in these little places could be good for us. We can talk a bit here, far away from politics and the hurly-burly of Paris. How is life with you?"

"It's killing me," Mauri replied. "I'm not up to the struggle. I'm going to tender my resignation as minister, then I'm going to do nothing, I shall just let myself die. If I felt strong enough, I'd be a genius; but my mind isn't in it, my heart neither. I am a seeker after Forbidden things. Happy the father who makes of his son his lover! A thousand times happy the son who becomes his father's mistress!"

"You love your mother. You are her lover!"

"By choice and inclination, yes; but no sacrilegious contact has defiled us, my dear Madame, because the law, to which I profess a profound devotion, forbids it. You are my wife, and I respect you. Oh, if not for you, the act would have been committed long ago."

She drank steadily; the saucers piled up in a pyramid and people were saying:

"She'll be getting soused again…"

"She's got another husband today."

And she confessed:

"Me, I have a passion for spirits. I feel happiest when I have a few drinks taken. Nothing gets my goat more than the sight of a teetotaller. I'd like it if the sea turned into Trois-Six de Montpellier: I'd drink the lot. Yes, dammit, the lot. And I'd drink the pebbles into the bargain. Don't snap at me, Noirof, I'm a good friend, but you shouldn't piss me off, dammit! I'll knock your block off. *Vive l'Empereur!*"

That was it, she was soused. In ten minutes she'd downed a litre of the hard stuff. One way and another he got her back to the Rue de la Plage, but there she refused to go any further.

"Let me be! Don't have me make a fool of myself. First of all, I'm sitting down."

She sat down on a bench.

"You're not going to spend the night there!"

"Got to sober up a bit; after that I'll toddle on."

"Where are you staying?"

"Don't remember. Fuck off will you, dammit, or I'll piladate... I'll dilapidate... I'll lapidate you with stones."

She picked up some stones and threw them about randomly. Someone came up to Mauri.

"Don't bother with her, Monsieur, this happens almost every day. We just leave her be, she unalcoholises of her own accord... and then starts all over again."

He wasn't staying here! Not with Hermine getting as drunk is this! Her, with her gooey eyes, the eyes of a doe in love, or the eyes of a ewe that's about to get its throat cut! She who made pellets out of her snot and ate them! He wasn't staying here. And anyhow, he was anxious to be on his way; he returned to the hotel, collected his offspring and, early next morning, got ready to leave. His room looked out over the lawn; he opened the window and leaned on the sill. Nothing, not a sound, a silence steeped in Boredom. Under his window, on the lawn which was no more than a vast stretch of short-cropped grass cropped extra-short by the fiery sun, were six cows, three fat and three lean. The latter were grazing, the former were not. The ones that were grazing seemed to be browsing on clods of earth, so short was the grass; the ones that weren't grazing were gazing, with eyes the size of a train's headlight, at passers-by passing by. But since no one was passing by, they were gazing at nothing.

Back in Paris, Mauri rid himself of his ministerial duties and then gave notice on his apartment in the Rue de Rennes. It was too costly for his liking; he wanted to live more modestly from now on. He spotted a little place on the seventh floor, in the Boulevard Saint-Michel, which he liked very much and agreed to rent. He drew up an inventory of his furniture. Never had he seen it so clearly, just lumpy blocks of wood the Blunderlander artisans had decorated here and there with crude rosettes and saints. The artists' genius had been inspired by the interiors of the churches and chapels of their home province, and these details they carved into the wood profusionally. The bed consisted of a large packing-case with an arched opening roughly cut into the top which, together with the curtains and beading, made it look a little like a puppet theatre, with the curtain bunched to the sides and its crude proscenium arch. The bed supported another one on top, which supported others in turn, like the bunks on a passenger-liner. The cook slept aloft, Noirof's stable-boy below him, the maid below the stable-boy, the cabby below the maid, and master and wife below the cabby. There was the traditional matching wooden bench for the bed. Then there were the tables, built like the chests for storing flour that Breton peasants eat their meals off, with no cloth on the lids, just the minimum of objects essential for their meal; then there were the benches for the dining-table, with their balustraded back-rests. Hermine was very attached to these benches, and at every mealtime without fail cried out: "*Tostaid ar skàon ouc'h aun daol.*" Finally, there were the Pont-Aven cupboards, chairs, chests, trunks and "*karr da neza*" spinning-wheels. It was all clutter, sucking up the air and stinking of decay. Paul-Uc-Zo-Émilie lay on the Kavel, with its honeycomb decoration and diamond-shaped inlays; the open-work moulding at the top gave it a vaguely Italian air and one really felt that Bonnat's *Scherzo* could easily have dozed in it.*

"I don't want all this stuff here any more."

The move kept him busy. One rainy day he went with the enormous removal-van carting his goods and chattels towards the Observatoire at the far end of the Boulevard Saint-Michel. Reaching the Luxembourg he caught sight of La Pondeuse accompanied by a friend; it was the *cocotte*, her unlucky partner in the game of manille they'd played long ago on the Rue Monge.

"You'll be wetting our whistles for us, won't you, dearie? We're dying of thirst. We're back from Bagneux* where we led the Eden's principal dancer to the kingdom of the worms. I'll be taking her place. So, you're no longer a minister?"

"No, I'm not."

"I used to say to myself: 'What's he doing being a minister? It's got to be some sort of mistake.' But there you are, what goes up must come down."

"A matter of luck," the *cocotte* observed. "Me, I'm out of luck. I haven't opened my legs in three months."

She was using a rabbit's foot to powder her face.

"This foot, Monsieur, came from one of the many who've given me the brush-off in the course of the last twenty years."

They went into the Closerie des Lilas, where nothing called to mind the romantic period of the Mimi Pinsons and the Schaunards.* In daylight dimmed by the café's leaded windows and the patina of the smoke-stained ceiling, where everything was steeped in melancholy, they sat round a marble-topped table while a real Breton storm was brewing somewhere nearby: "Christ! Jesus

Christ! Jesus bloody Christ! Jesus bloody Christ, Mary and Joseph!... jeez... jeez..." It was the proprietor, a prickly little fellow who was happier when in a rage. When he wasn't annoyed, nothing went right. At that moment he was pacing up and down in the cellar, all on his own, reeling off his repertoire of oaths like an actor rehearsing. As soon as he heard customers' footsteps he poked his head round the cellar-door, a bearded, moustachioed, porcupined head tufted with a forelock as stiff as a lightning-rod: "Waiter! Look sharp! Blast your eyes a thousand times, God damn it!" Then he went back into his hole and returned to his rehearsal where he had left off.

"Seeing as how you're moving, dearie, we'll give you a hand. But really, the weather's a bit dry: a person could still use a little something."

The removal-men were invited to join them for a drink.

"You there, I know you," one of them said to Mauri. "We had a bit of a knees-up that time with the ladies, it was around six in the morning in the Rue Campagne-Première. Ah, now that was some party! Not bad at all."

To pass the time, they played a game of skat.

"It goes without saying, we're not out on the town," announced the *cocotte*. "In any case, the removal-men aren't being paid to have fun."

"You're right there. We've got to be back before nightfall."

They abandoned themselves to endless card games. From there they went on to the Prado, back along the Rue Campagne-Première, carried on down the Boulevard Edgar-Quinet, paid their respects to the madam on the Boulevard de Montrouge, tottered along the Rue d'Odessa and ended up in the cellar-bar of the *Clémence Isaure*. The removal-van followed on. The whole party was a little drunk. They got the horses tipsy too, giving them six buckets of beer to drink. At the *Clémence*

Isaure La Pondeuse danced the *ré-la*, an *entrechat* newly created by herself at the Eden. And they drank copiously; the saucers piled up, reaching the ceiling. When the night ended, and they had to pay the bill, Mauri didn't have any money.

"I'll write you an I.O.U. ... payable within three months..." he lamely suggested to the proprietor.

"It's cash I want."

Nobody had any.

"Then leave me something in lieu, your watch, or a piece of furniture."

They agreed terms by handing over Hermine's own personal bidet. They had put away two hundred and twenty francs' worth of drinks; the bidet brought them fifteen louis.

"We can dine on the difference."

They went on down the Rue de Rennes and made their way to Les Halles. It was still raining; by opening their mouths wide and lifting their heads they could make believe the rain had turned into beer. The removal-van brought up the rear. The horses were laughing: they were drunk.

They went into the *Père Tranquille*. They ate like a pack of wolves, drank the very best vintages and drained carafes of champagne and chartreuse. By way of payment they had to give up one living-room and two bedrooms to the restaurant-owner. Their total came to eight hundred and one francs; the sale realised nine hundred and two. With what was left over they made their way to the *Caveau*. The van followed still.

"This place reminds me," said Mauri, "of my younger days in years past. I met lots of strange people, from hooligans to writers. It's all different now. Apart from ourselves, there's nobody left alive. That said, I'm a ruined man, well and truly ruined. All the better then; I want to reduce myself to absolutely nothing, so as to see what..."

They played the Destruction game. Using a penknife, they slashed their clothes until they were rags. When dawn came, they were sent packing and again, by way of settling up, had to leave behind three tables, six chairs, a bed and a comb. The rain was atrocious. They sought shelter in the market. They did a deal with a stall-holder, exchanging a mirrored wardrobe, a piano and the original plans for the L'Hay tunnel for a cartload of carrots. In the fishmongers' section they purchased fifty bags of mussels, a lobster and twenty baskets of mackerel with the remaining furniture from the van, which they piled into, perching on top of vegetables and fish. Then they set off for the Boulevard Saint-Michel. Crossing the Pont Neuf they were hailed by two very gentlemanly gents, themselves fairly drunk, who were harassing a couple of respectable ladies.

"Well now, it's the Bishop of Djurdjura and the Duc de la Croix de Berny!"

Mauri got down to shake hands with them.

"Everything's on the slide, old fellow," the Bishop informed him. "The place on the Butte aux Cailles has closed down. They overdid the high jinks, and the reserve fund was squandered within a fortnight. We had to mortgage it; the Duc has bought back our temple and has turned it into a baby-farm."

The Duc explained his plan:

"I welcome in any decent girls who come knocking on my door. I give them good board and lodging and so on and keep them there until thanks have been given for the safe birth of their babies; then I dismiss them, bestowing upon them the same prize as is given to the *rosières** of Nanterre. Naturally, all the infants must stay with me. My aim is to have a thousand children, then I'll retire from the business. At the present time I'm expecting sixty-nine."

Another old crony came by, it was the slap-artist.

"Oh, the shittiness of the inevitable, or rather the inevitability of shittiness," he whinged. "I've been relieved of my duties as lower-order executioner. Here I am, reduced to slapping myself about so as to make a living. Would you believe it, it only happened a couple of days ago. I had two executions on the go. 'Great,' I said, 'on with the show.' Splendid. I cut two centimetres off the first one. 'Careful,' I said, 'mustn't overdo it.' With the second one, I did him for eighteen centimetres. 'Bugger,' I said, 'that's my job gone.' And right enough, it was. This bloke went off and complained, and they decided in his favour. Would you like me to play you the Footsie-Footsie tune?"

When they arrived at the Boulevard Saint-Michel, the concierge objected to their moving in; of all Mauri's belongings nothing remained apart from his ministerial portfolio and the piece of brick, which he had kept as a relic. The removal-men asked for what was owed them, and so the food supplies had to be sold back to the local bistro-owners. With this deal Noirof made a slight loss of five hundred and four francs, twenty-eight centimes; but he still had two hundred and three francs plus a *sou*.

"I," he said, "fancy spending this in a way that is wholly original."

He went off to see the director general of the tramways company.

"It's raining, Monsieur," he said. "The mud is filthy and makes it hard to walk, your vehicles are under siege. Allow me, please, to annoy some of my peers. Put a tram at my disposal, on the route from Montrouge to Thermes, and back again. I'll pay you, at each stop, the fare for a full complement, but I alone will have the right to travel."

"By all means," the director replied, "with pleasure, Monsieur."

And slowly, this special excursion was undertaken; people came running up, and the conductor sent them on their way, pointing at the sign which read: "Full up". At each stop, Mauri paid 11fr. 70c. When the return journey had been made, he found himself back on the pavement — where should he go now?

He knocked on Madame Israël's door. With a threefold catch in her voice, she sent him packing.

"I only have an income of twenty thousand to live on, do you want to have me die of hunger?"

He set off in search of some furnished accommodation and, by chance, entered a house on the Rue d'Assas where a notice offered what he was after. As he was going in, he blundered into Hermine who, not wearing a hat and with a shopping-basket on her arm, was attending to her domestic chores.

"I thought you were with your mother, Madame."

"Imbecile!"

He didn't understand, and all of a sudden, paternal feelings began to churn his guts. His son, his four-headed son, where was he? Surely he hadn't sold him too with the odds and ends of furniture and vegetables? At a spindle-shanked gallop he headed for his former home. Paul-Uc-Zo-Émilie was lying in his own filth in a corner, howling fit for eight. He grabbed his son and ran to the Hippodrome, the place where he'd met the mother, and where he thought it most fitting for his son to have his début. This proposition suited the director, and Mauri put the little one on display. He suckled it. The Devil himself could not have had greater success. Mauri thought this was his salvation — he made fifty francs an evening, twice what Mani-Mina had been getting.

But Zo got whooping cough, Uc diarrhoea, Émilie sugar diabetes and Paul lupus. The four of them died together.

Mauri returned to his mother, with whom he was still madly in love.

"Let's make love," he implored.

"Not here, oh no, not here. Far away, if you wish, in the country."

And they left straight away.

Time, seeing nature all enamoured wanting child,
  Sows in the furrows Forgetting, when the earth is piled.
Though fixed on Death's axis, the wheels of Heaven turn.
  And April's smiles show all forget what they might learn.*

But it was a hard road. Dusty and shimmering, it threaded its way through the countryside studded with flowers in bloom like a myriad precious stones, threaded its way amid an excess of greenness. The landscape was becoming excessively green, the green dazzled, scarred, on the low ground and the high, by the dirty grey wall that ran round the park at L'Hay. Scattered here and there on the trees, among the pale hues of the early shoots, were the whites, reds and yellows of flowers whose balmy fragrance floated up into the sky. The Earth was making herself up and putting on scent like a tart whose flaccid charms needed this spicing up to give her some appeal; she had shed the stench of an elderly whore and was in full bloom, and lovers flung themselves upon her. She was hideously beautiful, just like a Woman.

And it was a difficult road. It rose steeply, like the road to Golgotha. Here and there it prickled with stony points that bruised their feet. It knew nothing of the touch of tender caresses; it made the ascent to Pleasure painful.

And it was deadly still, as still as the motionlessness of space. That

Sunday everything was at rest, man and all the elements of nature. Only the Bièvre flowed at the bottom of the valley, but silently, timorously, binding its impure molecules together as tightly as possible so that they made no sound in touching.

Slowly they climbed this Golgotha. His mother said:

"Look back."

He turned round.

"You misunderstand: look back at the past year. Have we experienced that special Sensation? It grieves me, Mauri, that you are a man of your times and nothing more."

The outline of the tunnel's chimney could be clearly seen, giving off plumes of black, very black smoke.

"The bowels of the earth are echoing with the vibrations of your discoveries; you have begotten a marvellous creature, but you have also loved in a thoroughly ordinary fashion! You have eaten the brains of dead men, but haven't grasped the symbolism of such a descration! Thus must I shape you, O coarse example of a man! Let us weep and rejoice, for today we shall join the Blessed of the Damned. If only man could one day know nothing of who he is! Oh, oblivion! Oh, recollection!"

She lifted up her skirts, indecently.

"I'm on fire. I want to drift on frozen seas. There's something really preying on my mind. I can see elephants flying — I see suns creep through the heavens, dark places become light! Oh, if one could but live life and die death! Hold, knights-errant of Oblivion! I see a leech waltzing on four feet, its hair blowing in the wind; with jaws of steel it crushes liquids and drinks down the stars... I think I have stopped being mad! Am I become wise?"

 She spat blood and her eyes were bloodshot too. She had the pale face of a virgin, and like a spectre, her huge body loomed above the endless dust upon the path.

"I see dark places become light. Can't you hear anything? Can you not make out that fantastic noise, that hurts the ears? It is the disintegration of the Great Whole. We ourselves are soaring. Beneath our feet mankind is dying out, and will always die, even after the skies of the East have lost their clearness, even after space has become solid. I shudder. I should like to write a novel, a true story in which I would inscribe our sublimities, O my son, in which I would set the vastness of the decomposition of our souls."

Like a spectre, her huge body loomed above the endless dust upon the path. She lifted her head, right up, up to the sky, higher than the sky, and from her bloodless lips there fell these words:

"Don't you hear anything? Does no strange odour afflict your sense of smell? I feel as though I'm fluttering in a red mist, above a sea of boiling blood, and that the scent of death's last agony permeates the mist. I smell death. At this moment a rotting human carcass is lying somewhere, I am breathing in its scent…"

Her quivering nostrils were dilated like those of a mare.

"… it is a scent that disturbs me, that intoxicates me, racks my nerves but to which I offer blessings because it revives me, purifies me, cleanses me. Let us hasten on. I am longing to consummate the Orgy, the great Orgy which cannot be in the eyes of God."

The valley was streaked with serried ranks of poplars, and as they climbed, the horizon by degrees expanded; depending on how the ground rose and fell, they could glimpse white gables, red roofs, odds and ends of sky. The elder trees gave off their fragrance, the same as a bed's in which an ancient virgin has lain for ten centuries without changing the sheets; the buttercups stippled the hillsides with drips of fake gold; the buds were dying, but not a single leaf quivered in the trees: the air had mummified, and did not move.

They arrived at L'Hay. They went into the church and prayed, surprised at how nondescript the place was.

"God isn't equally great everywhere. Otherwise all his houses would be alike."

A pictorial decoration in the sacred place portrayed the massacre of the innocents: swords blazed, ravaging their flesh, children with their bellies ripped open suffered in the agonies of dying, their features unsightly with pain.

"Imagine, all these brains and we haven't eaten any of them!"

As they went out they learnt that formerly there had been a cemetery on the site of the church. In the public square adjacent, a fountain was spitting from a lion's mouth crudely shaped in bronze its water which stank so foully that the inhabitants had to disinfect it before drinking.

"Oh, the country is dead hereabouts," a wine-merchant told them, "well and truly dead. There's nothing here, no industry, no commerce; walk round the village, you'll see only old people: no one is born here. All they do is die."

A slight breeze picked up. It was strong enough to stir the minute-hand of the church clock; a sparrow, always the same one, liked to perch on it. Before the half-hour, the hour-hand ran fast; by way of contrast, after the half-hour it ran slowly. In this way it was always on time in the final reckoning. Then it struck three precisely.

"The hour of Redemption! Let's hurry," she repeated. "Let us find a place where we can carry out the great Orgy."

As they passed by a farmhouse they heard cries of distress. Peasants both male and female came running up, and mother and son followed without thinking. They passed through a worm-eaten gateway, trampled across dung-heaps mushy with sump-water and found themselves in the middle of a courtyard cluttered with agricultural implements, their ears rent by horrible piercing shrieks.

"Murder! Help!... Help!..."

She, to Mauri:

"What was I saying? The carcass is here! The wine-merchant was right — all they do here is peg out."

He suggested:

"Let's go and see? It's always so pleasant to contemplate the suffering of others!"

And they climbed the farmhouse stairs. People were clustered together on the landing, staring at a door. The door, massive and bolted on the inside, was resisting the most strenuous efforts of the local authorities. The village constable, at the end of his tether, pressed his lips to the keyhole and said clearly:

"O you, who endlessly and so loudly proclaim the imminence of your demise, yet do not succeed in being murdered, which is a nonsense since, well, as long as you're bawling you won't have had to kick the bucket," (he said: keek the bocket) "if you want helping, come on then and open up. That's only reasonable, for crying out loud! Don't go losing your head!…"

The voice responded:

"How can I?… How can I?… He's throttling me…"

"Who are you? Man or woman?"

"Yes… Murder!… The tongue's sticking out…"

A tongue?

"Bastard!… Bastard… Help!…"

The cries became muffled: somebody was putting a spanner in their works.

The mayor girded himself with his sash of office.

"Open up in the name of the law!" (he said: lawer).

But nobody opened up.

"In that case," he declared, "let us confabulate together."

He turned to the local fireman.

"Someone smash a window, damn it!"

And the voice went on repeating: "Bastard!... Bastard!... Bastard!..."

The man climbed a ladder, fired something through the window, leapt into the room, unbolted the door, opened it, emerged, very agitated, then, gravely, with an ecclesiastical movement of the hands, said:

"Pray!"

The peasants understood; the men bared their heads, the bonneted women disbonneted, they made the sign of the cross, knelt down, while the mayor, having stepped two paces forwards, stepped back three.

"What horror is this?"

The voice implored: "For pity's sake!... Free me!"

"I recognise that voice," said Mauri.

And, resolutely, he went in.

On a very neat and clean bed, still not unmade, showing no sign of a struggle, lay two bodies, those of Hermine and Jardisse. Hermine was alive, Jardisse was dead. He was dead, with his arm around Hermine's neck. Death had come as he slept, and the cold on her neck had awakened the young woman. Upon opening her eyes, she saw a corpse and tried to free herself, but the arm's rigidity prevented this. Her head was locked in the fold of his elbow as if in a frozen vice, and the vice was slowly, gradually tightening. The two heads were looking right at each other, and were touching. The dead man's nose had shrunk somewhat; on the other hand, his tongue, defibrinated, stuck out, very long and very hard, and had entered Hermine's mouth. She had tried in vain to avoid this contact, but surrendered, despite herself, to its nauseating yet sublime caress. The tongue was oozing a gelatinous, yellowish, snailishly sticky wetness; in seeking not to taste the putrid

 staleness, mixed with the water-closetian emanations from the stomach, the unfortunate woman gasped, thereby allowing the organ free entry; but, soon tired, she closed her mouth again, thus imprisoning the vile object, ingesting it, sucking it, shifting it from right to left like an old tobacco-wad, swallowing its deathly juices. She tried to speak, but was choking. Then, driven to desperation, she lopped off the part with one bite, chewed it up and swallowed it. It was then that she cried out:

"Free me!"

But it was impossible to release her from the dead man's embrace. The arm was too rigid; they had to take a saw to it. And, while the fireman was cutting into the cold flesh, she confessed:

"Forgive me, Mauri. I loved him because he was a rotter. There's no helping it, life's full of contradictions. Why do they put windows in hospices for the blind? Why do they water the streets of Paris when it rains? Why don't they build public urinals in the cities for women to use? Why don't people in Clermont-Ferrand read novels?... I always loved him... I always lied to you... When I said I was visiting my poor people I was lying, I was going to see him at his place, on the Rue d'Assas, to see him, here, to see him, there; I drank absinthe with him, that's why I reeked of aniseed when I got back home to you... Your starchy foods didn't make me lose weight... Have them bury me in Père-Lachaise... What killed me was the tutu..."

And she repeated it: "Tutututututu."

The arm was sawn through.

She rolled on to the floor, quite dead.

When the body had been encoffined, they set off for Bourg-la-Reine station. The night was black. The road was easy. The countryside smelt pleasant. His mother said:

"Well then? Here we are, the blessed Delivery. Happiness always comes along eventually..."

At the station some young people were singing. La Pondeuse was there.

Mauri asked her:

"Just explain to me how there was light in a house with no windows. You remember — Messé-Malou?"

"Done with a systematic tilting of superimposed mirrors, dearie. Off you go now, your mother's staring daggers at us."

The train moved off. In silence their eyes, their wild eyes settled upon the coffin placed on the seat opposite them. They were alone. They understood each other. Abruptly, he seized her and bent her over the coffin. She abandoned herself. He abandoned himself. They abandoned themselves.

And they knew each other in a long, impure and hideous embrace...*

26 September 1891

⊁ FINIS ⊱

Page 21. Extracting gold from the paving-stones of Paris. The idea must somehow have been in the air, since it turns up again in an article Alfred Jarry contributed to the journal *L'Œil* of 24 May 1903, "Un Klondyke à Paris" (*Œuvres complètes*, II, 449-50). The annotators of the various editions of Jarry's works have not identified its original source, however.

24 Marriage *à la* Reclus. I.e. no legal marriage at all. Élisée Reclus (1830-1905), anarchist and distinguished geographer, founded the Anti-Marriage Movement in 1882.

25 Pompeux. Literally just pompous, high-falutin, but there is further word-play here too. *Pomper* is one of the many words for "to fellate", and a *pompeuse* is a prostitute who specialises in fellation. A *puceau* (two lines down) is a male virgin (so distinct from a *pucelle*), and in popular etymology a *puce*, a flea, would be the only likely visitor to such a person's pubic regions.

26 The Duchesse d'Orléans and the Electrice of Saxony. Elisabeth Charlotte de Bavière, Princesse Palatine (1652-1722), second wife of the Duc d'Orléans, brother of Louis XIV. Her letters, mostly written in her native German, show her to have been what the old *Oxford Companion to French Literature* calls "a woman of sturdy outspoken character". Elisabeth's aunt, Sophie of Hanover (1630-1714), was the grand-daughter of James I of England and the mother of Elector George who, in 1814, became George I of England.

27 Frottoir. Before the days of cheap and readily available wood-based paper, an arse-wipe cloth. **Switzer.** A Swiss mercenary soldier; the term carried a distinct implication of uncouth brutishness.

33 La Pondeuse. From the verb *pondre*, to lay eggs, and by extension, to breed, to produce. The English verb to punt and the noun punter are cognate with the French verb *ponter* — thus we may presume that the lady is an inveterate and reckless gambler.

34 Planter's chocolate. One suspects this is a contemporary allusion to anal sex. **Jean-Louis Forain.** Painter, book-illustrator and cartoonist (1852-1931), one-time drinking companion of Verlaine and Rimbaud. Famed for his sarcastic wit and, in old age, for his reactionary opinions and virulent anti-semitism.

35 **Francisque Sarcey** (1827-99) was the leading theatrical critic of the time; he was so influential he became a celebrity in his own right, but was heartily detested by many, including Zola.

36 **Charles de Brosses** (1709-77): apart from quarrelling with Voltaire (who remained aloof), one of the first to take an interest in "primitive" man in his *Du Culte des Dieux Fétiches* (1760); **Edward Burnett Tylor** (1832-1917) was a pioneer theorist of anthropology; **Herbert Spencer** (1820-1903), evolutionary thinker, effectively the founder of "Social Darwinism" and credited with inventing the word "sociology".

39 **Montrouge.** A southern suburb of Paris with a distinctly unsavoury reputation.

40 **Mary's month.** May, regarded as sacred to the Blessed Virgin Mary. The Romans thought May was unlucky for weddings since the festivals of Bona Dea, goddess of virginity, were held then.

43 **Brown-Sequarding:** boosting his sexual vigour with remedies invented by Charles-Édouard Brown-Séquard (1817-94), physician and physiologist, a pioneer of the then popular organotherapy, the famous monkey-glands, extracts from primates' testicles. Whether Leo XIII (1810-1903), Pope from 1878 until his death, benefited from the treatment is debatable. He did, however, establish various dioceses in Africa.

44 **Viollet-le-Duc and Garnier.** Eugène Viollet-le-Duc (1814-79), architect and historian of architecture, prominently involved in the restoration of Notre Dame de Paris; Charles Garnier (1825-98) designed the Paris Opéra, certainly the most opulent opera-house ever built. The **King of Bavaria**, Ludwig II (the "mad one"), was a generous supporter of Wagner and builder of extravagant fairy castles.

48 **Basilica at Montmartre.** I.e. the Sacré Cœur, begun in 1875 on the site where the Commune broke out, thus generally considered a symbol of the state's suppression of the revolutionary cause.

53 **Lustra.** In Roman reckoning, a lustrum is a five-year period of purification.

56 *Maison de tolérance.* The French name for a brothel.

59 **The Cirque Hippodrome** was an enormous building on the Boulevard de Clichy.

60 **Chez Maire**, on the Boulevard Saint-Denis, is described in old Baedekers as being "of the highest class".

62 **La Villette.** An insalubrious neighbourhood to the north-east of Paris, beyond

the Gare du Nord, at this date very much an industrial district. The gas-works were next to the railway line. A bit to the east stood the abattoirs and the cattle market, now the site of a science and industry museum and a park. **Magny's** (a few lines below), just round the corner from the church, was a "great" among restaurants, the meeting-place of the famous fortnightly dinners (1862-75) uniting Flaubert, Gautier, the Goncourts, etc. It was still going strong in the 1890s.

63 **Godard.** Towards the end of the 19th century there really were three balloonist Godards; in the absence of any forename, and in the present context, it seems likely this one was Louis, celebrated for his altitude-breaking record in 1900 of 8,538 metres.

63 **P.L.M.** The Paris-Lyon-Méditerranée express.

72 **The Panthéon** houses the tombs of the great and the good, from Voltaire and Rousseau to Hugo. **Saint-Lazare** (next line), a women's prison from 1811 to 1928.

74 **The Bal Bullier**, a dance-hall in the Latin Quarter, was a noted resort of students and bohemians. Old Baedekers note that "it needs hardly be said that ladies cannot attend these balls".

75 **Spinning-top:** word-play here on *qu'il ressemblait une toupie*, since in colloquial usage a *toupie* is not only a spinning-top but also a brainless old trout of a woman or a pliable individual who "spins about" at anybody's prompting.

98 **The Bièvre:** Paris's "other" river, which at this time threaded its way through the south-eastern suburbs to the Seine near the Jardin des Plantes, and was made stinking by the effluents from the tanneries there. It was celebrated in a long prose-poem by Huysmans that Genonceaux published.

100 **Vibrios.** According to *Chambers English Dictionary*, a bacterium of the genus *Vibrio*, having a slight spiral curve and usually one flagellum, as that of cholera.

108 **Deibler.** The Prisons de la Roquette, closed in 1899, on the Rue de la Roquette in the eleventh *arrondissement*, housed condemned men awaiting execution who were then publicly dispatched on the premises. Louis Deibler (1823-1904), commonly known as Dr. Deibler — his victims were his "patients" — served long and faithfully as the state executioner.

110 **T.H. Meynert (1833-92).** Pioneer neuropathologist and brain anatomist who in 1875 became director of the psychiatric clinic of Vienna University; believed that disturbances in brain development could predispose to psychiatric illness and

that some psychoses are reversible. Among his pupils was a certain Sigmund Freud.

114 We can perhaps recognise in this paragraph a sideswipe at the notions of interior décor to which many of the "decadents" aspired, and which had been most painstakingly described in Huysmans's *A Rebours* (*Against Nature*), an author Genonceaux had published.

116 A famous murder case. This crime was widely and salaciously reported in the contemporary press, which dwelt in detail on the grotesque circumstances and catalogued the various exhibits mentioned, which were employed as depicted in the illustration here. The perpetrator, Michel Eyraud, was guillotined by Deibler in February 1891 on the Place de la Roquette. Souvenir vendors circulated among the crowd hawking tiny replicas of the famous trunk containing a minute corpse. Eyraud's accomplice, Gabrielle Bompard, received a twenty-year prison sentence.

118 From the Comte de Lautréamont, *Les Chants de Maldoror*, Canto III, 4.

120 From *Maldoror*, Canto IV, 8.

122 Angelus. In Roman Catholicism a prayer said at 6 a.m., noon and 6 p.m. (announced by church bells), celebrating the Incarnation and the Annunciation, and beginning with the words *Angelus Domini nuntiavit Mariae* (The Angel of the Lord declared unto Mary…).

125 Charlotte Corday (1768-93) stabbed Jean-Paul Marat (a deputy of the National Convention during the French Revolution) to death in his bath on 13 July 1793. She was guillotined, rather promptly, four days later.

126 Catchpole. Archaic term for a constable, a petty officer of the law — in the

French text the similarly archaic *happe-chair*.

127 *Ora pro nobis.* Pray for us.

127 Sardanapalian. Sardanapalus was the Assyrian king (died c.620 BC) celebrated for what dictionaries call his "effeminacy" and love of luxury.

128 Sesostris. According to Lemprière's *Classical Dictionary*, "the age of Sesostris is so remote from any authentic record, that many have supported that the actions and conquests ascribed to this monarch are uncertain and totally fabulous". **Jan Memlinc** (c.1433-94), a founding father of Flemish painting, whose works include a *Last Judgement*.

129 Antoine Vollon (1833-1900), is described by the *Petit Larousse* as a "genre" painter "of rare vulgarity". **Bernard Palissy** (1510-90), founder of French art pottery, died in the Bastille, an unrepentant Huguenot.

130 Repopulation. An allusion to the widespread fear, stoked at the time by hyper-nationalists after the defeat of 1871, that the motherland might lack soldiers able to combat the threat from a similarly nationalist Germany. Procreation was of course a cause enthusiastically espoused by the Catholic Church.

133 Dome of Les Invalides: the church attached to the home for old and disabled soldiers founded by Louis XIV. It houses the tomb of Napoleon as well as numerous French generals. Concerning this toilet in Piccadilly, Antony Clayton, author of *Decadent London* (Historical Publications, 2005), was kind enough to offer these comments:

If we assume that the American Bar mentioned is the one at the Criterion during that period, then according to a map of 1880 in Hermione Hobhouse (*A History of Regent Street*, Macdonald & Jane's, 1975, p.75) the toilets were directly opposite on a traffic island. The London Pavilion was over to the right and Eros on another island to the left (it's since been relocated). In Michael Harrison *London Beneath the Pavement* (Peter Davies, 1961) I found the following description of the "underground urinal at Piccadilly Circus" on p.258:

"This was a place in the grand manner — architecturally speaking — and must have gladdened the heart of the connoisseurs of such places. One descended to it by a precipitous flight of iron steps and, long before one entered the rotunda, one was aware of it by a curious smell of hot carbolic — or of carbolic-flavoured steam. All the stonework of the stalls was of some pinkish, marblish stone, and the water to flush these unseemly halting places was held in reserve above one's head in vast glass-walled tanks, held together at the edges with brass strips, half polished with Bluebell [a popular metal polish] and half coated with verdigris. Not infrequently a wag used to introduce a gold-fish into a tank. It's not important, but all the metalwork was vast and complicated, in the most aggressive aspect of Marzipan; and all was painted a shiny aluminium."

At that time Piccadilly Circus was notorious as a hangout for prostitutes.

135 The tenth Muse: a rank often bestowed on the great poet (and supposed author of *The Tutu*) Sappho. Her affectionate relationships with her female friends are well attested in her works. Less certain is the legend about her suicide, leaping into the sea from the cliffs of Leucas, inspired by an unrequited passion for a young boatman called Phaon.

146 Carpeaux. Jean-Baptiste Carpeaux (1827-75), prolific sculptor, noted for his skill in depicting groups of figures. The reference here is presumably to his *Les Quatre Parties du monde*, right enough in the Luxembourg gardens.

148 Panclastite. A liquid explosive of the period, based on hydrogen peroxide and picric acid, invented by the chemist Eugène Turpin. The term, a Greek-inspired neologism meaning something like "all-destroyer", dates from c.1890 and must have appealed to Genonceaux, whose taste for that sort of thing was marked.

149 *Stat crux dum volvitur orbis.* The Cross is steady while the world is turning.

149 FH. Fire hydrant.

155 Léon Bonnat (1833-1922), "official" portraitist of society ladies and of several presidents of France. At the height of his career he commanded fees of thirty to forty thousand francs. His painting *Scherzo* (1873) is a sentimental genre piece depicting a woman, perhaps a gypsy, and a laughing young girl.

155 Bagneux. Parisian cemetery.

155 Mimi Pinsons and Schaunards. Mimi Pinson is the eponymous heroine of a story by Alfred de Musset (1810-57), a delightful and kindly *grisette*, or dress-shop girl, and the prototype of the consumptive Mimi in Murger's 1851 novel *Scènes de la vie de Bohème* (and of Puccini's 1896 opera). Schaunard is the musician who wanted to warm Mimi's tiny frozen hands to life.

158 *Rosières.* According to widespread, especially rural custom, those girls of sixteen who had remained virgins would be awarded by the local authority a wreath of roses, a minuscule dowry and sometimes a ceremonial carriage-procession. Baedeker and Muirhead guides record that, at Whitsuntide, a *rosière* ceremony was held in Nanterre, then still a village close to Paris, until the early 1920s.

161 Verse translated by Chris Allen.

168 This last sentence deliberately echoes, but also deliberately differs from the crucial phrase in *Les Chants de Maldoror* (II, 13) which tells of Maldoror's sexual encounter with the she-shark: "… *ils se réunirent dans un accouplement long, chaste et hideux!*" (they were united in a long, chaste and hideous coupling!).

For a complete listing of all titles available from Atlas Press
and the London Institute of 'Pataphysics see our online catalogue at:
www.atlaspress.co.uk
To receive automatic notification of new publications
sign on to the emailing list at this website.
Atlas Press, 27 Old Gloucester st., London WC1N 3XX